Liberty Frye
❀⚜ and the ❀⚜
Witches of Hessen

OTHER BOOKS BY J.L. McCREEDY:

Liberty Frye and the Sails of Fate (Book Two)

Liberty Frye and the Emperor's Tomb (Book Three)

The Orphan of Torundi

BOOK ONE

Liberty Frye
and the
Witches of Hessen

J.L. McCreedy

PENELOPE PIPP PUBLISHING

Published by Penelope Pipp Publishing

www.penelopepipp.com

ISBN-13: 978-0-9882369-1-2/ISBN-10: 0988236915 (pbk)
ISBN-13: 978-0-9882369-0-5/ISBN-10: 0988236907 (ebook)
Library of Congress Control Number: 2012915902

For Sam, who told me to follow my bus.
Thanks for never giving up.

CONTENTS

CONTENTS

ᶜWARNING

his is a tale about a remarkable girl who is forced to face unimaginable things. It should not be read by those who despise anything out of the ordinary, who disapprove of smart (and somewhat stubborn) young ladies, or who disdain any hint of adventure. Nor should it be read by those who believe that the world around them is as it seems, because at least in this case, it definitely is not. No, *this* tale is filled with treachery and mystery and with exploits so daring that only the very stalwart should dare to read. And so, if one should find this document and feel compelled to proceed, it is strongly advised to do so with caution, in a supervised manner, and no matter what, never, ever read this tale within one hour of eating.

1

THE DARK STRANGER

Delbert Snookles was a man who enjoyed his whisky. Especially on Sundays, when the streets of Baluhla, Mississippi, were quiet, without a car or person to be seen. It made it far less likely for him to trip over things and almost impossible to get into a fight.

On this particular Sunday, Delbert tottered about town with his bottle, smiling at nothing in particular. After all, he was relieved just to get out of the house. His wife Ernestine drove him nuts, and that kid Ginny who was staying with them made him downright uncomfortable. So, like any reasonable man, he'd made up some excuse about checking on something at his shop (he owned a feed store on the town square) and then quickly left before Ernestine could express her disapproval.

"Women," he grumbled. "Can't please 'em for nothing."

Delbert took another swig and was just about to enjoy a nice, relaxing afternoon under an oak tree by his store when he heard a strange voice from behind him say:

"Pardon me."

It was such an unexpected sound that Delbert nearly choked mid-swallow. He spun around to observe an unusual looking gentleman standing before him. Delbert noticed that the stranger was quite thin, and he wore a dark suit and black polished shoes that perfectly matched his dark, beady eyes. The man's straight, black hair was slicked back from his face, showing skin so pale that it practically glowed in the sunlight.

Creepy.

"Shouldn't sneak up on folks," harrumphed Delbert, trying his best to appear unfazed. "Never seen the likes of *you* in these parts before. What's your name?"

"Please excuse my inconsideration." The stranger smiled, showing sharp, little teeth. "My name is Iorgu and I'm a bit lost, you see. Would you happen to know where I might find the Frye residence?"

Delbert Snookles hiccupped and wiped his nose with the back of his hand. He'd never heard of such a ridiculous name. Iorgu, indeed. But the man looked well kempt, so he couldn't be a bum or a criminal, at least not one from these parts. Maybe he was a strange relative of that wife of Peter Frye's, he considered. After all, wasn't she from Germany or Romania or some such far-flung place? He decided it wouldn't hurt to answer.

"There's two Fryes around here," he informed the stranger. "Do you want the family near town or the old kook in the woods?"

The man named Iorgu thought about this for a moment, and then he said, "I believe it would be the family near town."

"Well, don't know why you'd want to find *them*; they keep to themselves, strange if you ask me," sniffed Delbert. "Unless 'course, you're after that bread she delivers. Don't know if the missus does business on Sundays though, but if you must, you'll find their house down that-away." Mr. Snookles waved an unsteady finger to the south, where a dirt road wound out of town. "Can't miss it this time of year; has a tree right in front." He paused to take another swig. "Bright red."

"And just to be sure I have the correct residence, they do have a child, don't they, perhaps around ten years of age?"

Delbert snorted with obvious distaste. "You mean that girl of theirs, Liberty Frye?"

"Why, is there something the matter with her?"

Delbert scratched his chin thoughtfully as he frowned off into the distance. "Well, not in the technical sense of things. She's just … *different*."

"Oh? In what way?"

"Can't explain it exactly," grumbled Delbert. "But weird things always happen whenever she's around, and I'm not just talking about the fact that she don't act like other girls her age," he paused, shaking his head in disapproval before concluding: "Makes me uneasy."

"I see …."

"Lately, she shows up at my shop, wanting to buy stuff for that pet goose of hers," continued Delbert, warming to the stranger—it was nice to meet someone who took an interest in things, after all—and then he offered his bottle as a token of appreciation, but Iorgu politely declined. Delbert shrugged and took another swallow. "She's always usin' funny words like 'comestible' or 'delectation.' I mean, how's a man to even know what she's talking about? I don't have nothing like that in *my* store. And you should see the way she dresses, too. Peculiar-like. Wears things in her hair and funny clothes from the consignment shop. Once, she showed up with a top hat on that noggin of hers. When I asked her what for, she said that she was exercisin' her creativity! Should be 'shamed of herself, that one—downright unladylike to be using highfalutin words and exercisin' creativity and the like."

"A true travesty," agreed Iorgu.

"Poor parenting, that's what it is. Why, Ernestine says that a young lady ought to know better than to act different than everyone else … it's plain inconsiderate!"

"Indeed," nodded Iorgu.

Delbert grunted in response, and then he thought of something else that bothered him, but before he could say anything, the stranger had turned and was now walking down the road he'd pointed to earlier. Delbert watched after him a moment, frowning. It made a man wonder what the world was coming to when strangers with names like Iorgu just showed up in the middle of one's Sunday, wanting to know directions to the most unvisited house in town.

"No telling," he concluded blearily, and he was just about to get himself situated under that oak tree when the strangest thing happened. The man he'd been speaking to suddenly turned into a bird, right in the middle of the dirt road. No, wait. *That* couldn't happen ….

Delbert rubbed his eyes and then examined the label on his whisky bottle. When the words came into focus, he decided everything looked about normal. Yup. Same brand he'd grown to know and love for years.

"Nonsense," he growled, looking back at the road. But sure enough, nothing was there. Nothing but a huge, black bird—a raven, to be exact—soaring up, up, into the blue, summer sky.

The raven circled above the little house with the odd, fire-red tree just in front. Down below, it made out the form of a girl perched on one of the tree branches, with bare feet dangling from the boughs, reading a book with an unusual dark green binding.

The girl held the book with both hands, her face bent intently over the wide pages, squinting through an antique pair of horn-rimmed spectacles that didn't appear to actually have lenses. She looked around ten years old; she had springy strands of light brown hair escaping from the floppy cap on her head—and remarkably large feet. When she finally looked up for a moment, her light hazel eyes glowed in the sunlight, reflecting a golden green.

"Liberty Frye," a voice whispered from the sky.

Libby didn't notice because she was happily reading a gruesome story involving the amputation of toes—an activity she found especially helpful in forgetting depressing things such as the fact that her weekend was almost over. In fact, she was so engrossed in all of the gory details that for the moment, she didn't hear her pet goose, Buttercup, honking in sudden distress from below, his wings flapping angrily at the dark creature soaring above Libby in the sunny, September sky.

The raven ignored Buttercup and continued to circle above, swooping in every now and then to catch certain details of Libby's face, of the little house, of the voices and sounds inside where Libby's parents were having coffee.

The raven's sharp eyes suddenly noticed a figure approaching from the road; it appeared to be another girl, carrying a package wrapped in newspaper, and she was walking toward Libby's tree with a strange expression. Quietly, quietly, the raven circled down to the roof, hiding behind a gable, and watched as the girl grew nearer.

"It's not safe up there," called the girl as soon as she reached Libby's tree. The tone of her voice held a tinge of annoyance, as though she found it highly inconsiderate for someone to be lounging in a tree on a Sunday afternoon.

Libby started in surprise and nearly fell off her branch. Luckily, one of her unusually large feet caught between two limbs, giving her just enough time to catch her balance and scramble back to a sitting position.

"You should at least be wearing a helmet," the girl continued to lecture. "Did you know that falling from trees is the second biggest cause of death for children from unintentional injury in the United States?"

Well, Libby had to admit that she didn't. But she *was* curious to discover who had walked all the way over here just to prattle off injury statistics, so she peered between the boughs and discovered a chubby girl with big brown eyes, freckles and a very tight ponytail glaring up at her. She'd never seen the girl before, but there was something about her that seemed ... sad, Libby thought.

The girl instantly looked away.

"Did you know that, from the road, it looks like your tree is on fire?" she asked in that same demanding voice.

"Now *that,* I was aware of," grinned Libby. "Isn't it wonderful? My mom calls it the *Baum des Feuers.*"

The girl frowned.

"It means Tree of Fire," Libby explained. "She's German. She's got funny names for everything. Anyway, she says it's some kind of magic tree—that it holds a special power."

"What ... kind of power?"

"That's the problem," admitted Libby, leaning back on her branch. "No one knows. I tried to make a tea out of the leaves once, but it only made me throw up. Although I *did* feel a little tingly afterwards."

The girl stared up at Libby in a manner that suggested she questioned her mental stability, but after a while, she asked in a slightly less uptight voice, "What are you reading?"

Libby turned the book so that the cover tilted toward the ground, displaying ornate, gilt letters that flashed in the sunlight.

"*Fairy tales?*"

"Vintage Grimm Brothers," corrected Libby, laughing as Buttercup flapped up to where she sat and nestled in beside her. "They're very interesting—totally different than anything you'd expect. And besides, it's the only way I can have a decent adventure. My parents are super strict, so I have to live vicariously."

The girl frowned again, clearly disapproving of anyone who lived vicariously—especially through vintage fairy tales in a bright red tree, no less.

"But what about you? What brings you here?" asked Libby.

The girl tossed back her head. "You know the fancy, white house next to the Baptist church?"

"Sure, the Snookles." Libby nodded, because she was far too polite to say anything else, even though Mr. Snookles was probably the rudest store owner in town. Worse, she knew that Mrs. Snookles still hadn't paid her mom for that fancy birthday cake she'd made last year.

"They're my aunt and uncle," the girl continued loftily. "My parents are away on important business, so it looks like I'll be staying with them for a while. Anyway, I suppose fifth grade here is as insufferable as anywhere else."

"Hey, I'm in fifth grade, too!" said Libby. "I can show you around if you like—maybe we can hang out and stuff."

"You probably already have lots of friends," replied the girl.

"Not exactly," said Libby, feeling her cheeks grow hot. "I mean, when the most popular girl at school makes fun of you all the time, it sort of limits your options. But my mom and dad say it's just a phase," she quickly added. "And my Uncle Frank says it's because I actually have a personality."

"Most people don't admit to that," the girl mumbled, and then she turned to go.

"Hey wait!" called Libby, leaning out from her branch. "I don't even know your name. I'm Libby, by the way. Libby Frye. What's yours?"

"Ginny Gonzalez," the girl said. "You really should consider a helmet, you know."

And with that, Ginny walked back towards town without so much as waving goodbye, her tight, pink dress slowly blending with the dirt road. Libby watched after her for a moment, still hanging from her branch. With her free hand, she pushed back strands of hair that had stuck to her forehead.

"Strange girl," she muttered.

"Hey Sassafras," her dad called from the house. "How about those math drills? You promised we'd finish them up after lunch, remember?" The sound of his voice disturbed something on the roof, and Libby looked up to see a huge, black bird lifting into the sky. She shook herself, feeling a peculiar prickle down the nape of her neck.

"Okay, Dad," she sighed, tucking her book under her arm. "Down in a minute."

❀❀

From a quarter of a mile away, Ginny walked toward town with her newspaper package. She stopped for a moment and looked behind her; from where she stood, she could still make out the red plume of foliage that marked where she had thought she had seen a fire. She stared toward the tree with her dark, somber eyes.

"Strange girl," she said.

2

THE YELLOW ENVELOPE

The raven swooped over the town of Baluhla, soaring far above the treetops. Its wingspan stretched to at least seven feet and created a shadow over the whitewashed building being used as the fifth grade classroom. With an odd grace, the bird floated toward the roof, stretching out its talons, one of which clutched a thin, yellow envelope.

"Kraa kraa," the creature rattled.

Its eyes glittered with eerie intelligence as it perched above the schoolroom, scanning the horizon dotted by oak trees, old farmhouses and piney woods. Its wings trembled slightly from the sudden sound of the school bell ringing, followed by the double doors flinging open, spilling out children in various stages of motion.

The raven continued to crouch, disinterested in the activity below, until it caught sight of Libby hopping down the stairs.

"Toc-toc-tok," the raven said, and the glint of its feathers flashed blue and purple in the sunlight as it lifted into the sky.

❀

Libby hadn't made it very far down the road towards home when she saw two boys just below the hill where she stood. They appeared to be dragging something into the woods.

"What do you want?" came a wail. "I won't say anything, I promise!"

Libby instantly recognized Ginny's voice. She'd wondered what had happened to her after school; she'd never even had a chance to ask her how her first day went, although after yesterday, she wasn't entirely sure if Ginny even wanted to speak to her. Well, she sounded like she was in trouble, Libby decided, so she hurried down the hill anyway, quietly following them into the woods.

"What a wimp," snorted one of the boys. "C'mon Ginny. Aren't you happy to see your new cousins?"

"Please, just let me go," whimpered Ginny, but this just made the boys laugh even louder as they took turns shoving her to the ground. From where Libby crouched, she watched angrily, trying to think of what she should do. And then, before she realized what she had decided, she was swinging her backpack around and stepping into view.

The two boys slowly turned toward her.

"I hate bullies," announced Libby, trying to sound unafraid, but her heart was beating so loud she was sure they could hear it.

"Look, Ron, our little cuz has got a friend," sneered the first boy.

"Cute one, too, but feet like Sasquatch," added the other, and they both started laughing again, which was all the incentive Libby needed.

"That's a big word for you," she smiled sweetly, pulling something out of her backpack. It looked distinctly like a slingshot.

The boy called Ron stopped laughing and stepped toward her instead, his eyes narrowing, but just then, a bright blurry object flew through the air and smacked him squarely on the nose.

"What the—" he yelped, clutching his face.

POW!

ZWEE!

ZOW!

ZAP!

PANG! Came a sixth, and by then, it was a purple massacre. For just a second, Libby froze, shocked by her own accuracy. Both Ron and the other boy were folded on the ground, their heads tucked under their arms.

"Please just stop … we'll leave you alone," whimpered the one boy, and Ron mumbled something in agreement. Ginny coughed, reminding Libby that she should probably say something.

"Then get out of here, and don't you ever mess with my friend again!" she commanded in her most intimidating voice, but it came out more like a squeak because in truth, she was pretty rattled. She'd never hit anything more than a tin can before in her whole life!

The boys groaned in response, which must have sounded defeated enough to convince Ginny to get to her feet. She stumbled toward Libby, her eyes as big as paper picnic plates.

"Holy Macaroni! Did you just *shoot* them?"

Libby nodded, grabbing Ginny by the arm and trying her best to continue out of the woods as calmly as possible, but her legs felt like they'd been zapped by a liquefier. Ginny didn't seem to notice.

"With ... what?"

Libby dug into her backpack and displayed a large, purple berry in the palm of her hand. "They're from my tree," she managed to say.

"Berries and a-a slingshot?"

"You never know when it'll come in handy," noted Libby, carefully placing her weapon back into the left pocket of her bag. "Of course, I use it for defensive purposes only ... don't tell my parents."

"I-I think you're my hero," wheezed Ginny, her eyes still so wide it looked as if her sockets were expandable. "No, you're my *superhero*."

Libby laughed at this, which immediately made her feel better. It also helped that she saw Ron and his friend limping off in the other direction, bedecked with peculiar, purple splotches in some very unusual places.

"Who are those boys, anyway? We ought to report them!"

"They're Mrs. Snookles neph—er, my cousins," Ginny quickly replied. "I wouldn't worry about it—they'll be gone in a couple hours anyway. They're just mad because I saw them smoking."

Libby thought about this as she glared after them. Something about it all didn't add up.

"And I'm sorry for being rude to you yesterday," Ginny added.

"Oh! Well, it's got to be hard being new," shrugged Libby, starting to smile. "Besides, I thought you were … informative."

"Thanks, but I was rude," said Ginny, and then she stared awkwardly down at the ground.

"Hey, why don't you come wait it out at my house?" Libby suggested, unsure of what else to say. "You should try some of my mom's cookies; she's a professional baker, you know. Everyone says her baking makes them feel better—it'll fix you up in no time!"

Ginny looked dubious, but she nodded gratefully. "Well, if you're sure it's okay."

"Perfect!" grinned Libby, and as they headed down the road, Libby turned around one last time, just to make sure they weren't being followed. But the two boys Ginny claimed as her cousins were nowhere to be seen. In fact, there was nothing to be seen at all except a gigantic raven circling far above them.

The raven looped in the sky once more and then, with a loud caw, it darted on ahead, still clutching the yellow object in one talon.

❋

When Libby and Ginny arrived at the cheerful little cottage with the bright red tree in front, Libby's mom was standing in the open doorway, holding an envelope in one hand and a rubber spatula in the other.

"Uh, oh," Libby whispered, walking slowly toward the porch steps. "She looks really mad—even her hair looks angry."

"Do you think this is some kind of a joke, young lady?" snapped Gretchen Frye from where she stood waiting, and Libby glanced at Ginny with a stunned, how-could-she-know-already look.

Ginny shook her head, her eyes growing large again. "I think I should go," she whispered, but Libby was dragging her up the porch steps and introducing her, all at the same time.

"No way. Mom, this is Ginny! She's new."

"Nice to meet you," said Ginny, who didn't seem too sure about that, but before she had a chance to make a run for it, Mrs. Frye had tucked her spatula into a pocket and was shaking her hand.

"Nice to meet you, too," Mrs. Frye said while staring furiously at Libby. "Normally, I'd be in much better spirits to meet a new friend, but right now, I'm particularly displeased with my daughter. Now, I've asked you a question: do you think this is some kind of joke?"

Libby shuffled uncomfortably and glanced between Ginny and her mother.

"What? Am I embarrassing you?" continued Mrs. Frye. "You should have thought about that beforehand, shouldn't have you?"

Libby threw an apologetic glance at Ginny, but Ginny just looked bewildered, probably too busy having her arm pumped up and down to notice much of anything else.

"Well, I don't know what to say, Mom. I-I only used it because …."

"It was self defense! She saved me!"

Mrs. Frye blushed and immediately released Ginny's hand, which disappointed Libby a little, because, despite the humiliating circumstance, she couldn't help but admire her mother's endurance. Must be all that whisking, she considered ….

"She really did! I would've been toast otherwise," continued Ginny, now rubbing her shoulder.

Libby threw her a grateful smile. "Well, I wouldn't say *that*, but I really wasn't going to use it—I had it in my bag just in case, you know, and good thing too because, as it turns out, I—"

"What are you *talking* about?"

Libby and Ginny exchanged more glances. "Er, the slingshot, Mom. You're mad because Dad made me swear I wouldn't take it to school or … or actually … um, *use* it on anyone."

Libby's mother took a deep breath, closing her eyes for a moment.

"I thought you had lost your slingshot."

"Right," said Libby, and then she took a great interest in the buckles of her cloth Chinese slippers.

"However, the slingshot is not the topic of this discussion."

"No?" squeaked Ginny.

"No," confirmed Mrs. Frye, staring once more at Libby, and her voice was low and slightly trembling. "Because right now, I'd like you to think of something else that you might recall. Vhy do you think I am upset vith you, Libby?"

Libby continued to examine her shoes for a few more seconds before meeting her mother's gaze. She was about to point out to her that she was pronouncing her "w's" with a "v" again, but decided against it.

"Okay. I remember now. Is it that spider in your q-tip jar?"

Gretchen Frye took a tiny, sharp breath.

"Because that's for a psychology experiment. His name's Oscar."

"*No!*" Mrs. Frye scowled as she whipped the yellow envelope into the air. "I mean *this*, Libby! H-how could you? And, how could you even know about them to *do* this? Just to leave something like this for me to find on our front step! This is nothing for you to make jokes over! You've no *idea* how this affects me."

Libby stepped back and held her hands up in protest. "I don't know what you're talking about, Mom, I swear," she said as earnestly as possible, but this had the opposite effect she had hoped for. Her mother's lips tightened in the way they always did whenever she was trying not to lose her temper, and her face grew very pale.

"A lie is a dangerous thing, Libby."

Libby thought this was a little dramatic, especially over an envelope.

"But I'm not lying."

Her mother blinked.

"You're certain?"

Libby nodded, not knowing what else to do. She'd never seen her mom look so suspicious of her before, not even when, in the middle of last year's Christmas cantata, Mark Shaw's choir robe had mysteriously fallen apart at the seams, revealing him in nothing but a dress shirt and polka-dot underwear, right when he started his solo. How this was possible, the good people of Baluhla Baptist Bible Church still marveled, but it *had* happened, even though, of course, Libby couldn't possibly have had anything to do with it ....

"Just like last week, when your dad tried to take your slingshot away so that you wouldn't bring it to school anymore and you swore up and down that you had lost it?" her mom was saying, and her voice was a little too calm.

"Well, I *had* misplaced it—" mumbled Libby, but she could see that this time, whatever her mom *thought* she had done, it was something far worse than wishing a mean boy's choir robe would disintegrate ....

"Or yesterday evening, right after you promised us that you would go to bed by 9:30 for school nights and I found you hanging upside down in your tree at exactly 10:55?"

"Yes, but, it was for educational purposes. I was reading about bats!"

"They sleep in the *daytime*," Ginny whispered.

"Not all kinds do!"

At this, Gretchen Frye arched an eyebrow, and although she still looked very stern and had her hands folded in front of her, there was a little twitch at the side of her mouth that fought off a smile. Libby looked up at her mother hopefully, but not for long, because then her mom said, "Please go to your room. I need to talk this over with your dad vhen he gets home."

"But that's not fair!" Libby protested. "I don't know anything about that letter, so why do I have to go to my room?"

"I have my reasons."

Libby felt her face burn hot. "You always have your reasons, but you never tell me what they are!"

Mrs. Frye frowned and looked away. "It is for your own good, Libby. Someday soon, things will make more sense. I promise. Now, please do as I ask."

"Oh, fine!" Libby swallowed hard and stomped into the house, knowing it was no use. Her parents were constantly doing things like this, and it drove her crazy. Always overreacting to every little thing, sending her to her room when the slightest event out of the ordinary occurred, as if her room held some kind of a magical barrier to the world outside. It was so unfair! And it was always, "Someday soon you'll understand," or, "We'll tell you as soon as possible," and the worst one of all was her mother's favorite: "We're only doing this because we love you." She hated it!

❀

Now as a general rule, Libby was an exceptionally good-natured individual, and it never took long for her to get over her anger. In fact, by the time she reached her room, she felt considerably calmer. She also realized that Ginny was still trailing after her.

"Sorry about that; and sorry you didn't get any cookies," she muttered sheepishly.

"It's okay, I tend to comfort eat anyway," said Ginny. "But you sure do a lot of things to get into trouble. Maybe you should try following the rules."

"Maybe if they stopped treating me like a zoo animal, I would," Libby grumbled as she opened the door to her room. She watched as Ginny immediately walked towards an enormous world map painted on one wall, highlighted with dots.

"You've got a lot of dots."

"Future adventures," said Libby, cheering at one of her favorite subjects, and she pointed to a ceramic cow on her book shelf. "I'm saving up. My Uncle Frank's traveled everywhere, and he says it's the best education you can get. Besides, my parents met in Germany—my dad was in the Army—so I figure I'm bound to travel by the very nature of my existence, even if my parents are determined to keep me in my bedroom for my entire life."

"Well, travel can be quite dangerous. I prefer to simply read about places; it's much more hygienic. Got internet?"

"No way," replied Libby in disgust. "Like I said, they're super strict."

Ginny looked around the room and then settled onto a

cushion on the floor. "Too bad. We could've done some research on yellow envelopes. You know, maybe the color has a meaning. Any idea who might have sent it?"

Libby shook her head, growing irritable once more at the thought. It was just one of the many things about her parents that didn't make sense. She had no idea who would have sent it; her parents never got letters, except a few Christmas cards and stuff from one or two people in town.

She'd always thought it was strange; her parents never spoke about anyone—much less wrote letters—and no one outside Baluhla (except Uncle Frank) even knew who they were. It was almost, Libby had often considered, as if they were hiding from something, but that was silly. Her parents were the most boring, law-abiding people she had ever known. What could they possibly be hiding *from*?

Frustrated, she walked over to the window. Just then, a dark cloud passed overhead.

"Looks like a storm," called Ginny.

Libby looked glumly outside, sighed again, and grabbed a basket full of purple berries from the windowsill. She walked back over to Ginny and plopped down beside her. "Well I guess we can work on this necklace for Buttercup if you want …."

But the darkness that Libby had mistaken for a cloud was, in fact, not a cloud at all, which just goes to show that when a girl assumes things, she can miss out on some pretty important information.

For instance, in this case, the cloud Libby *thought* she saw was actually the shadow of the raven settling into the boughs of her tree. From its perch, the raven watched the two girls in the room—its gaze specifically fixed on Libby. If one listened very closely, one just might hear the low rumble of something. Something that sounded like a voice. A *human* voice coming from the enormous raven in Libby's tree.

"And so it is done," the voice said. "Liberty Frye shall soon be in our grasp. At long last, I may return to my master."

And then, the raven lifted its wings and flew away.

3

THE MYSTERIOUS
ANNOUNCEMENT

ays had gone by since the incident with the letter. Libby's mom had never spoken of it since, except to apologize the next morning for blaming her, which of course drove Libby nuts. Her parents simply refused to talk about it, offering annoying, cryptic responses that they loved to give, such as, "We haven't decided yet, but we'll tell you when the time is right."

Naturally, Libby decided to take matters into her own hands. She searched the house from top to bottom, trying to find that yellow envelope, but her mother must have eaten it, because it was absolutely nowhere to be found. She and Ginny even cleaned out the entire pantry in search of a cookie tin

Libby knew her mom hid important correspondence in—it took a lot of persuading on Libby's part to get Ginny's help— only to be rewarded with some recipes that called for weird spices she'd never heard of and a bunch of sappy love notes written by her father. It was embarrassing for everyone.

More time passed by and before long, Ginny spent so much time at Libby's house that she was practically a member of the family. In fact, Libby's parents began to worry it might be offending the Snookles. Ginny assured them that they didn't care, which appeared to be true since Mrs. Frye had asked them over for dinner several times, but the Snookles always refused with an air that made clear they had no intention of actually getting to know the family that Ginny spent so much time with.

It was strange, Libby thought, and stranger still was the fact that Ginny never spoke about her parents, or where they were or when they were returning from their mysterious trip. It seemed like everybody had secrets—everyone, at least, but her ….

Soon, it was November, and Uncle Frank's birthday was coming up that weekend. Libby could hardly wait for Ginny to meet her eccentric great uncle. Libby loved every moment they spent at his dilapidated house in the woods. Just getting there was a minor adventure; the unmarked, pot-holed path branching off the main road thirteen miles out of town was actually his driveway, and it curled and twisted another three quarters of a mile before any hint of a house could be seen. It was definitely remote, overgrown, difficult to reach and a little bit creepy.

In other words, it was exactly how Uncle Frank liked it.

That Saturday afternoon, the Frye's station wagon turned down the driveway and rattled through the trees, towards a surprisingly well-groomed clearing that marked the lawn of Uncle Frank's house. The house itself loomed at the far edge so that, while Uncle Frank's front porch faced the huge yard, the back of his house met the wild and untamed growth of the woods. Tendrils of kudzu vines and wisteria curled along the sides of the white, Victorian-style structure, like a python in the process of swallowing its prey.

"It looks like it should be condemned," Ginny observed as the station wagon shuddered to a stop. "Isn't it a code violation or something?"

"Uncle Frank's a code violation," chuckled Libby's dad. "I love the man to death – he raised me since I was a boy and he's like a father to me—but still, he drives me crazy. He won't let us help him with *anything* and the stuff he does scares me half to death sometimes. It's impossible to keep up with him."

"He's really a genius—wait until you see the mobile unit he invented!" Libby added, but Ginny didn't have a chance to ask what that was, because the Fryes were already clamoring out of the station wagon. They marched toward the front steps of Uncle Frank's porch and then froze, staring down at an enormous hole that had swallowed up the center.

Ginny looked worried.

"Is that ... normal?"

"Define normal," said Mr. Frye.

Just then, the door to Uncle Frank's house groaned open. Libby's dad shook his head and frowned to himself, following the girls around the porch hole, through the doorway and into the foyer. They all stopped upon the black-and-white checkered floor and looked around. There was no sign of Uncle Frank.

"Do we go up *there?*" Ginny asked, pointing fretfully at the dilapidated staircase that wound up to the second floor.

As if in response, a crash resounded from somewhere above. A puff of smoke oozed over the second story landing and down the stairway. A few moments later, a seated figure appeared who, inexplicably, began moving down the rickety staircase without ever actually touching the stairs.

"And *that,*" grinned Libby, "is Uncle Frank."

As the smoke dissipated, Uncle Frank came into view, his eyes darting about the room, as if alarmed by everything that they saw, and his thinning, wiry hair stuck untamed about his head like long, brown and silver springs. (Libby suspected that Uncle Frank secretly dyed his hair—his only vanity, as far as she could tell.) He had on a mahogany-colored robe that looked as though it would have been worn by an ancient Turkish prince if it were not so threadbare and tattered, and best of all, he descended upon them in his mobile unit, apparently updated to include some sort of hover device, allowing him to float down the stairway with ease.

Before Ginny recovered long enough to list all of the safety violations she'd just witnessed, Uncle Frank was landing his mobile unit in front of them.

"Welcome!" he shouted.

"So now, we're levitating?" frowned Libby's dad, but Uncle Frank ignored him.

"Who's the intruder?" he demanded instead.

"This is my best friend Ginny, Uncle Frank. Remember? I've told you all about her—"

"P-pleased to meet you," Ginny said.

"Well, that's something I haven't heard in a very long time," chuckled Uncle Frank, which was definitely true. Most people were downright terrified to meet him, but in any case, no one was ever *pleased*. "Any friend of Libby's is a friend of mine."

Ginny smiled nervously and pointed to something that looked like an exhaust pipe sticking out between the upturned wheels of his chair. "Isn't that dangerous?"

"Well now!" Uncle Frank beamed in approval. "You're a question-asker. I like that! Means you've got hope for yourself! And of course it's dangerous—I call it my hover vent. It enables my mobile unit to convert between power sources, thus allowing the unit to temporarily suspend in air while manipulating over land-born obstacles."

"He means the stairs," whispered Libby, noticing Ginny's blank expression, but Uncle Frank was still speaking:

"You see, a typical mobile unit is useful only when it is confined to its traditional purpose, which, quite impractically, is to traverse the flat ground. What good is that, I ask you? Indeed, I asked myself just this question, and then I answered it by way of this invention, which, as you can see, enables me to climb and descend stairs, and even float up to a chandelier in order to change a light bulb, *if* I were so inclined, which I am not."

"Perhaps it can also float over to a phone so that you could call us when you have a hole swallowing up your front porch?" Libby's dad suggested.

"Oh, that." Uncle Frank waved a dismissive hand. "That was just a little experiment gone awry. Not to worry, Peter, I'll have it fixed in no time … besides, I don't have a phone, as you yourself are so fond of pointing out."

"So anyway," interrupted Libby's mom before they had a chance to quibble over the matter, because every time they visited, they almost always got into a disagreement about Uncle Frank's self-imposed isolation, "we have come to celebrate your birthday!" she announced cheerfully, holding up a chocolate cake.

"Excellent, excellent," cried Uncle Frank. He pushed a button that lowered his wheels back into the normal wheelchair position, and then he pressed another that whizzed the contraption towards a doorway leading into the living room. "Your baking always makes me feel years younger, Gretchen! Let's celebrate in here," he called behind him, and without waiting for a reply, he instantly took up a conversation with his nephew who had followed him into the room.

Libby busily poked a box full of birthday candles into the cake, but from where she stood, she could hear Uncle Frank shouting incomprehensible things like "quartic polynomials!" and "quantum entanglement!"

"How old is he, anyway?" whispered Ginny.

"Over ninety, but he won't tell us," said Libby, jabbing in a final candle.

"He doesn't *seem* that old."

"Are we speaking of his appearance or maturity level?" laughed Mrs. Frye, who was now walking with the cake towards the living room, where, incidentally, its occupants had suddenly grown quiet.

In fact, Libby hadn't heard Uncle Frank or her dad say anything in over a minute—a very peculiar thing, especially since whenever those two got together, they constantly argued or, on the off-chance they actually agreed on something, engaged in loud conversation. Everybody knew that Uncle Frank was a little hard of hearing (a slanderous rumor, in Uncle Frank's opinion), and so the silence made Libby suspicious.

She followed quickly after her mother and good thing too, because as soon as Gretchen Frye stepped into the room, she made a funny, squeaky sound, staggered backwards, and would have dropped her beautiful, triple-layered chocolate mousse cake had Libby not been there to steady the platter.

"Gracious!" she yelped, and the commotion shook some sense into Libby's father, who, until then, had been staring stupidly in front of him.

"Look, Gretch," he stammered. "Uncle Frank has invented a robot!"

Libby could hardly believe it herself, but there was no denying the aluminum, four-foot tall robot—complete with a broom and one of Uncle Frank's aprons tied about her little waist—standing in the middle of the living room.

"Indeed. Indeed, I have," grinned Uncle Frank proudly. "It's taken me over five years to get her the way I wanted—you should see her prototypes up in the workshop! She is my newest and greatest creation, and, sorry to say, the cause for the front porch's demise." Uncle Frank cleared his throat and looked around the room. "But that is another matter. Peter, my boy, you'll never have to worry about me again! Esmerelda will be able to cook, clean and bring me whatever I need, whenever I need it! She'll be able to speak, too. Who knows, in time, she might even recite Shakespeare!" His eyes glittered at the thought. "Of course, she's still a work in progress, but, then again, aren't we all?"

"Holy Macaroni," whispered Ginny.

"Cake?" beamed Uncle Frank.

Libby nudged her mother's elbow.

"Oh. Right," jumped Mrs. Frye, setting the cake onto the coffee table with concerted effort.

It took longer than normal for her to light all of the candles because she kept burning her fingers in the process, but as soon as she managed to get to them all, everyone sang *Happy Birthday* to Uncle Frank, he blew out the candles and then proceeded to chop up the cake without taking another glance at Esmerelda, as though it were a perfectly ordinary thing to be celebrating one's ninetieth-something birthday with family and a newly invented robot.

After everyone had eaten and watched one of Uncle Frank's favorite Charlie Chaplin movies, he wheeled himself over to Libby. "I've got something for you, kiddo," he said, rummaging about in a pocket beside his arm rest. "I made two, thinking you might have a friend to share with. Little did I know I'd have the pleasure of meeting her today!"

And then he produced two objects from his pouch that looked a lot like walkie-talkies.

"Thanks, Uncle Frank!" said Libby, hardly believing her good fortune, but her parents were already exchanging worried looks.

"Are those—" began Libby's dad.

"Oh, relax, you two, I know your rules, and these are no ordinary walkie-talkies. While they were indeed purchased at your local electronics store, I have installed a special wavelength and frequency modulator tied to a barometric and hydrometric sensing unit, thereby allowing these everyday-looking portable radios to optimize their signal according to real time and local atmospheric conditions, resulting in an extraordinary increase of their effective range."

"So you're saying that no one else can listen in on them?" pressed her dad and Libby scowled, hoping they weren't going to put the kibosh on this, too. They'd always been strict, but still, this was ridiculous.

"Not unless I make another one," harrumphed Uncle Frank. "They are independent communication devices capable of sending and receiving sound exclusively to each other at distances far exceeding regular range."

"You mean it's like a super secret cell phone?" Libby asked hopefully.

"Better," grinned Uncle Frank. "These work without any service charge. You can use them anywhere, anytime you want and it won't cost you a thing besides a battery! Of course, unless I make another one, they'll only work with each other, but that was the whole point, really—"

Click! Click!

A sharp knock from the front door interrupted Uncle Frank's explanation, which was just as well because no one would have understood it anyway. Libby scrambled to the foyer, followed closely by Ginny.

"Wait!" commanded Uncle Frank, wheeling his mobile unit behind them. He raised his hand, pushed back the sleeve of his robe, extended an index finger and pressed a shiny brass button on his right armrest. The front door swung open on its own. Uncle Frank, Ginny and Libby all peered out of the door to discover who the visitor was.

"This is most unexpected. I never have any visitors, scared 'em away years ago," Uncle Frank declared with some sense of accomplishment, and indeed, there was no one to be seen. Just then, a peculiar noise blared from behind them.

"Honk!" came the noise again, and the group spun around to find an indignant goose with a chain of purple berries around its neck standing in the foyer.

"Buttercup!" gasped Libby, scooping him up in her arms. "He must have flown here after us!"

"Is *this* the tiny gosling we found in the woods?" asked Uncle Frank in amazement, and Libby nodded, placing him on the porch.

"He's certainly imprinted," Uncle Frank marveled. "Thirteen miles is quite a distance to follow!"

"Imprinted is an understatement," chuckled Libby's mom, joining them. "You can't find a more educated fowl in Baluhla! He's been thrown out of fifth grade ten times and even has the distinction of getting kicked out of a movie theatre once, although what my daughter was doing at a movie when she was supposed to be with her youth group, I'd *still* like to know," she finished a bit huffily, but Libby was relieved to see that no one seemed particularly interested in that last bit, because Uncle Frank was too busy studying Buttercup, and her dad was concentrating on navigating around the porch crater to get to their car.

"I hate to do this, but we'd better get going," he announced as soon as he'd safely reached the other side. "Ginny's supposed to be at the Snookles today before five."

"Yeah, just so I can help them with their stupid dinner party," muttered Ginny under her breath.

"But before we go, we've got some news we wanted to share."

"What's that?" asked Uncle Frank, looking up distractedly from Buttercup, and Libby looked up in surprise, too. Her parents exchanged glances.

"We wanted to tell you as soon as we had decided on it," her mom began. "So … well, this Christmas, Peter, Libby and I will be going to Germany for a few days," she finished quickly.

"*What?*" Uncle Frank exclaimed, and Ginny poked Libby in the ribs with a why-haven't-you-told-me-this glare.

Libby's dad cleared his throat. "Gretchen's father—his health is failing. We received a letter; we don't know *how*, but somehow, they managed to find us … and his last wish is to see Libby, to see us all, for Christmas."

"I have a *grandfather?*" said Libby in disbelief.

"Have you forgotten?" wheezed Uncle Frank, and his hands gripped the armrests of his chair, accidentally pushing the brass button, which made the front door swing open then shut several times. Buttercup, who had taken to examining the porch area, squawked in perturbation as the door swept him back and forth. "Have you forgotten that you were almost killed?" continued Uncle Frank, his voice shaking as he spoke. "That-that … woman almost—"

"No, Uncle, we haven't forgotten," cut in Libby's dad, throwing Uncle Frank a significant look that made his mouth clamp shut, "but it is what we have decided we must do. To make things right."

"It's only for a few days," added her mom.

Uncle Frank said nothing, but his face was ashen.

"We'll be alright," smiled her mom, bending down to kiss his cheek, and then she turned and walked toward the car. Ginny followed nervously behind. "Let's go, Libby."

Libby turned to Uncle Frank, hoping for some explanation, but now his head was bent low so that she couldn't see his expression. Even so, he seemed to understand.

"It's not for me to explain, kiddo," he muttered darkly. "This is between you and your parents. You'd better get going."

Libby didn't know what to say; it felt like a big bucket of sewer water had just been dumped over their perfect visit, and on Uncle Frank's birthday, no less! She hugged him goodbye, not knowing what else to do, and then she picked Buttercup up from the doorway. Silently, she walked around the porch, down the stairs and crawled into the station wagon.

"What's going on?" she asked as soon as she hit the seat.

Her mom settled into the front. "All in good time, Libby," she replied without turning. "We will tell you what you need to know."

"Like the fact that I'm ten years old and just finding out that I have a grandfather?"

"Yes," answered her mother, and her voice was unusually tight. "You also have a grandmother for that matter, and there is a very good reason for all of this."

Libby gulped and turned speechlessly to look at Ginny, who was staring between Mr. and Mrs. Frye, her eyes wide and slightly alarmed looking.

"But it can't be helped," her mom continued, almost as if she were speaking to herself. "We're going to see them, and afterward, we'll explain everything."

"How about explaining now?" wailed Libby. "You always talk about the truth, and this whole time, you've been lying to me! What kind of family hides grandparents from their own kid?"

"How about changing your tone, young lady," replied her dad, sliding behind the wheel.

"And we haven't lied—we just haven't told you everything," added her mom. "Meet them first, Libby, then we'll talk."

With that, the car doors slammed shut, as if indicating by

their sound that the conversation was now officially closed. The station wagon rumbled to life.

As it rolled down the long driveway, Libby swallowed hard, feeling angry and hurt. She'd always thought her grandparents were dead, and here she was, ten years old and just finding out! And if that wasn't bad enough, she had obviously been blamed for that letter sent by them, and no one had bothered to explain anything for months!

It was just like everything else they did: secretive. And smothering. Never allowing her to do anything and never taking the trouble to explain why. But it was more than that, too. Something about it that she couldn't quite place, but she felt it, and it made her uneasy, even frightened. And the worst thing of all was that she knew there was nothing she could do about it but the thing she hated to do the most:

She'd just have to wait.

4

THE MOONSTONE AMULET

November faded into the cool days of December, and before Libby knew it, Christmas vacation was upon her. Tomorrow, she would be flying to Germany with her parents, still without a clue as to what that letter had actually said or why it was all such a big secret in the first place.

"We'll tell you as soon as we get back from our trip," was all that her parents would divulge. No amount of sleuthing had made the mystery any clearer, except to discover that there had been an unusual gentleman asking about town for the Fryes at some point in the past.

That afternoon, Libby and her parents drove to Uncle Frank's house for one last visit before leaving. They brought Buttercup along, with a list of instructions for his care while they were gone.

"Make sure you keep him on a leash when he's outside, Uncle Frank. Buttercup tends to wander off a lot," Libby reminded as Uncle Frank eyed her pet skeptically. She stood in front of his miniature Christmas tree, hooking a few ornaments on its branches while Buttercup hovered beside her, his head cocked to one side as if critiquing her handiwork. Uncle Frank shifted in his mobile unit, lifting his eyes to the sky.

"I have flown planes, fought wars and loved a beautiful woman," he lamented. "And now, look at me: I've been reduced to walking a *goose.*"

"Don't forget you're also a world-class inventor. Maybe you could invent something for Buttercup like you did for Esmerelda!"

"Just what I need: a chattering robot and a talking fowl."

"We'll only be gone for five days," laughed Libby. "Besides, you're the only one who can take him. Ginny already asked the Snookles and they told her no way."

Mrs. Frye muttered something under her breath as she carried a bag of groceries into Uncle Frank's kitchen, which sounded a lot like "intolerable people" and then, in a louder voice, she asked, "Libby, do you know why she stays with them? I mean, where are her parents?"

"Nothing wrong with being raised by one's aunt or uncle," cut in Uncle Frank indignantly. "After all, I didn't do such a bad job with Peter, if I do say so myself. Better than that lousy sister of mine who just dumped the poor kid on my doorstep …." Uncle Frank took a deep breath, as if trying to rein in his words, and just then, a cuckoo clock in the hallway struck six. Libby listened as the metal bird made out of recycled soda cans started its bizarre crowing; it had been one of Uncle Frank's very first inventions.

"You're all set for the holidays, Uncle Frank," called her dad, poking his head out of the kitchen door, and for some reason, this announcement made Libby feel depressed.

"I wish you didn't have to spend Christmas all alone," she frowned.

"Alone? I've got Esmerelda, haven't I? She can talk my ear off at this point, and besides," Uncle Frank added philosophically, "when your mind is full of ideas, you're never really alone."

Libby thought about that for a moment.

"Almost forgot! I've got something for you," he said, handing her a small silver box. "It's your Christmas present. Go ahead. Open it."

Libby took the box, feeling ridiculous, because her eyes were suddenly watering. "I don't want to leave," she realized out loud. "I wish I could stay here with you instead; I don't want to go to Germany."

"What!" Uncle Frank exclaimed, lifting up her chin so she had to look at him. "*You* don't want to travel? Foolishness, if I ever heard it! After all these years complaining that your parents never take you anywhere, and now you finally get the chance, and you're morose about it?"

"But it's not the same," protested Libby. "And besides, you don't want us to go, either."

But Uncle Frank was waving a dismissive hand, and smiling a little too lightheartedly in Libby's opinion. "I'm just a grumpy old man who doesn't like to see the only people he likes leave for a while," he replied with a chuckle. "Now, do as I say and not as I do, and for starters, you can open that box."

Libby felt confused by Uncle Frank's sudden change of heart, but she didn't want to seem ungrateful, so she opened her present and then lifted a sheer, metallic satchel that lay just underneath. She pulled apart the strings.

A smooth, flat moonstone, the size and shape of two pennies put side by side, and the color of indigo blue mixed with wispy swirls of white, fell with a silvery tinkle into the palm of her hand. Attached to the top of the stone was a metallic clasp, threaded by a chain of the same platinum color. Libby lifted it up, letting it dangle from her fingers: it was unlike anything she had ever seen.

"This is a very important amulet," said Uncle Frank, taking the chain and fastening the clasp behind Libby's neck. "More important than you can ever imagine. I want you to promise me that you'll never take it off. When you come back from your trip, I'll tell you all about it."

Libby stared down at the stone.

"What's the matter, don't you like it?"

"I love it," she gulped. "It's just that, it's so fancy. It's too special for me."

"Wrong there, kiddo. You're far more special than any necklace!"

"If by 'special' you mean different, then I guess," mumbled Libby, feeling even more ridiculous and confused; she quickly wiped her eyes and then turned the stone over in her hands.

Sometimes, it felt like Uncle Frank was the only one who understood her, and the thought of being away from him during their favorite time of the year was unnerving, especially under the circumstances. "I mean, school's bad enough, but even Mom and Dad treat me like there's something wrong with me. Just like this trip; it's like they've hidden me from my grandparents all this time, like there's something about me that they're ashamed of."

Uncle Frank considered her for a moment, his eyes crinkling at the sides, and when he spoke again, his normally gruff voice was warm with feeling.

"Firstly," he said, re-arranging her cap so that it tilted to the side at a jaunty angle, "there is nothing the least bit wrong with you. Your parents love you more than anything, Libby, and they couldn't be more proud. I have a feeling that when you get back from Germany, things will make a lot more sense. Your parents have a good reason for all of this, I am certain. ...." Libby opened her mouth to say something, but Uncle Frank held up his finger. "Secondly—and this might be the more salient point—of course you are different! All the most wonderful people are; it's what makes you the most alive!"

Libby frowned, not quite understanding what he meant by that.

"You just keep being yourself, Libby," concluded Uncle Frank. "It's the most important thing you can do."

"You've got a funny way of seeing things."

"I'm almost always right. Just ask your dad!" chuckled Uncle Frank. "And I want you to keep that necklace on you at all times. In fact, why don't you just slip it under your shirt while you're in Germany; I wouldn't even show it to anyone if I were you. That way, it'll be protected and won't snag on anything."

"Thank you," she said, feeling very strange all of the sudden, but she did just what he suggested, placing her hand over her shirt where the amulet now lay. "Merry Christmas, Uncle Frank."

Uncle Frank didn't reply at first, but continued to study her from under his bushy brows, and as Libby peeped up at him, she noticed something unusual in his expression....

"Yes, Merry Christmas," he finally said, but in a tone that almost sounded like a question. "I certainly hope it is, Libby."

❧

Libby was still thinking about Uncle Frank's strange goodbye when, hours and hours later, they finally arrived in Germany.

She followed her parents through the Frankfurt airport, her backpack feeling heavy on her shoulders; in addition to its usual cargo, it also held her walkie-talkie and the massive Brothers Grimm book that, for some reason, her mother had insisted they bring along. It probably had something to do with the letter she had never been allowed to read, she reflected grumpily, and she was just about to ask her dad if he would carry it for a while when she grew distracted by a wall plastered with snapshots that looked out of place for some reason. Before she could really inspect them, she was being

CHAPTER 4

tugged by her parents into the lobby and then out of the arrival doors.

"Taxis are this way," said her dad, taking her by the hand.

"You mean, they're not even going to pick us up?"

"Oh, no, your grandmother doesn't drive," answered her mom, and then she began exchanging words with a cabdriver with bewildering speed. Libby realized it was the first time she'd ever heard her mother actually hold a conversation in German, and it was strange to see someone so familiar in such a different way, almost as if it were another person altogether. Libby picked out a few words she could understand, but mostly, she just felt overwhelmed.

After the bags had been placed in the trunk, the family crawled into the back seat and sat huddled together as the car rolled down the road and sped onto the autobahn.

Libby craned her neck to see a blue sign swish overhead. "Hanau, 35 km," it said.

She watched as skyscrapers blurred past the walls of the autobahn, the tidy cars speeding along beside them, and the long, dark stretches of road that curled out in every direction, winding to towns and cities listed on neat, evenly spaced road signs. Her parents looked out the other window, and it seemed to Libby that her mother drank it all in, like someone who hasn't eaten in days and is suddenly surrounded by a feast, her beautiful, violet eyes pouring over everything they passed.

"Welcome home," she heard her father whisper, and her mom nodded distractedly in reply. Soon, the streetlights and tall buildings became less frequent, and when the walls of the autobahn were low enough to see over, Libby saw stretches of farmland with smaller towns dotted here and there.

"Maybe we should stop at the Hanau market and check in on Wolfgang," her dad murmured. "What do you think, Gretch?"

"But we haven't told her yet," her mom whispered back.

He father laughed, kissing the tip of her mom's nose.

"I think the fact that we've had a letter delivered to our doorstep more or less indicates it's no use hiding."

"Peter, not now!" She glanced over at Libby, who pretended to be deeply interested in something stuck in the rubber trim of her window. "Yes, you're right, of course ... but let's see Father first, then we'll go."

Libby bit her lip in disappointment, hoping they might say something else, but her parents had grown silent once more. She continued to gaze out of the window, feeling that familiar twinge of resentment. It was so unfair, all the secrets. They treated her like she was a baby, incapable of understanding the truth. Incapable of understanding *anything*.

And Libby couldn't have foreseen it, of course, but very soon, and under very different circumstances, she *would* understand. And the truth would be something she would never have imagined, not in a gazillion years, and more than that, it would change her life ... forever.

Forty silent minutes later, the car wove through the woods and stopped in front of an old, half-timbered house. The paint on the outside was chipped away, exposing patches of brick and sandstone between the remnants of dark green, and wide, dark straps of timber that sagged under its weight. In front of the house, a narrow bicycle path paralleled the tiny yard, disappearing once more into the woods a few feet beyond.

"Well, here we are," Libby's mom whispered, and her voice wavered strangely.

Libby stared at the old house, for the first time feeling that she really was here, in Germany. It looked just like the houses she had seen in pictures—only a little less quaint and kept up—and there were no other houses to be seen around it, just woods, which was not quite the German-village-scene that she had expected, but still, it looked like it had come straight out of her Brothers Grimm book.

With a nervous smile, she thought that it was the kind of place Uncle Frank would appreciate, with its sagging beams and chipped paint; only, there was no Uncle Frank or silly robot or anything else cheerful, for that matter. She felt Uncle Frank's necklace resting on her chest, and the thought of it gave her some comfort. At least she had that with her.

The sound of the taxi driving away distracted her from her reverie. She turned to her dad, who was picking up the suitcases with a rather dour expression. Libby couldn't see her mother's face, because she was clutching Libby tightly by the shoulders, her fingers pressing in so hard that Libby was just about to complain that her right clavicle was in serious danger of being crushed when the sound of a door squeaking open turned her attention to the front porch.

She looked up to see a short, stout woman with white curls and a pinched nose standing in the doorway, a steady smile spread across her face. And then, Libby noticed her eyes: a shade of light blue that somehow looked slightly dimmed, as if a cloud of fog had mixed into the blueness and had faded them. Even so, the color was striking, and as she gazed at what she supposed was her grandmother, she could not help but notice that, while her grandmother's mouth was smiling, those still, blue eyes did not share in its warmth.

"Mother," came a hoarse whisper over Libby's head.

"Hello, Giselle," said her dad, and with suitcases in each hand, he marched up the stairs, on to the small porch. He put the suitcases down. And then, with what seemed like a tremendous amount of effort, he outstretched his hand.

Giselle shook it nervously, her mouth moving in an odd sort of way, but she didn't speak.

"And this is Libby," Libby heard her mother say. "Libby, greet your grandmother."

"Hi," Libby squeaked, holding out a sweaty hand.

"After all of these years," murmured Giselle, looking down at her. "And I see you have your father's nose …."

"Yes," said her mom, placing her hands back over Libby's shoulders. "I am sure Libby is just as happy to meet you, Mother, but I think she is really rather tired. Perhaps you could show us our room now and, on the way, lead us to Father?"

"Your father? Why, dear, he stepped out for a bit. I am sure he'll be back soon."

"*Stepped out?*" said her mom. Her parents exchanged looks. "I thought he was …."

"Dying?" suggested Giselle. "Well, he certainly is, Peter, he certainly is. Given up any hope, the doctor has. But, in these last days, who can begrudge him a little exercise?"

Libby's parents stared back at her in disbelief, and for a split second, Libby had the feeling that something awful was about to happen. But then, her grandmother smiled again and bustled them across the front porch before anyone had the presence of mind to say anything else.

"I'll show you your rooms," she announced cheerfully.

"Actually, we would prefer to share the same room, all three of us," her dad replied.

"The same room? Why, how ridiculous! We have plenty of space for Libby to have her own!"

"All the same, we will be staying together," came her dad's response, and Libby looked up in surprise from her parents to her grandmother, not knowing what to expect next.

"Very well," her grandmother replied in a tone that made clear it would not be *her* fault, thank you very much, if this Christmas turned out to be an unpleasant one. "Please follow me."

Libby was vaguely aware of being led into the house, the smell of stale air hitting her the moment she walked through the doorway. She held her mother's hand tightly as her grandmother led them through the kitchen and down the hallway. Several furry creatures scattered here and there as the party progressed.

"Cats," her mom muttered.

Giselle stopped in front of a door and opened it. Inside, there was a double bed accompanied by one nightstand and a wardrobe. A bookshelf stuffed with old, dusty books provided the only other furnishing.

"But this is Father's room," her mom said. "Vhy don't we stay in my old room?"

Giselle regarded her daughter for a long moment before her face softened into a smile. "Tisk, tisk, Gretchen," she said sweetly. "All this time in America and you still cannot say your w's properly."

Her mom blushed.

"Never you mind that, dear. Klaus hasn't used this room in years; and as for your room, we've sold the bed and everything, so you wouldn't even recognize it. Now come, dear, I am sure Libby is very tired, as you said."

Libby wasn't tired at all. She was, however, desperate to get away from her grandmother, and she was relieved when her dad mentioned something about an extra mattress and disappeared with Giselle back down the hallway. Libby's mom wandered over to the bed and sat down.

Meeeeooooooww, a perturbed howl came from under the bed, and a charcoal-colored cat darted out of the room. Her mom stared blankly in front of her, not even noticing.

"Maybe I'll radio Ginny," said Libby, trying to keep things cheerful. She swung her backpack around and pulled out the Grimm Brothers book, placing it on to the white, crocheted bedspread.

"If it works," said her mom absently, and then she took to trailing her index finger around the gold embellishments of the book's cover, a slight frown hovering over her brow.

Libby reached into her bag again and pulled out her walkie-talkie, silently calculating the time difference. Uncle Frank had told her she'd be seven hours ahead, so it should be about nine in the morning in Baluhla, Libby decided. She pressed the button.

"Ginny, are you there?"

No reply.

"Ginny, are you there? Over and out," she called again. She waited about twenty more seconds; static crackled from her walkie-talkie, but still, no reply. She decided to try again later, walking over to the window instead. She peered out of the cold, filmy glass. It was only a little past four o'clock, but already, it was nearly dark. "It's so gloomy," she complained.

Her mom looked up distractedly.

"It's just the vinter—I mean, winter, darling," she said, and it seemed like she was making an enormous effort to concentrate on the present. "In the summer, it is like another world altogether. You would love it, Libby: it is green and beautiful, flowers are everywhere and it stays bright until as late as ten o'clock! I can just see you driving us crazy about bedtime," she smiled, and Libby realized she hadn't seen her mom smile like that in a very long time—maybe since that day she'd found the letter. "But even now, while it is dreary out, they have the most wonderful Christmas markets. Maybe we can go to the one in Hanau while we're here."

"Oh, can we, please?" cried Libby, jumping at the suggestion. "Besides, we have to get some presents for Uncle Frank and Ginny!"

But her mother didn't respond. She just sat on the bed with perfect posture, hands folded in her lap, now staring at nothing in particular. Libby looked into her mother's troubled, pretty face and knew that her thoughts were years away, somewhere in the distant, secret past that Libby had never known.

5

THE TERRIBLE TRUTH

By the next day, it was clear that something was horribly wrong. For starters, her grandfather had yet to make an appearance.

At first, it was the walk, and then it was a phone call saying he had to stay with a friend in town for the evening because he was feeling too ill to make it back home. In the morning, it was a slew of doctor appointments, and by the evening, her parents were so agitated that Libby half expected her mother to break into hysterics.

She wasn't far off the mark.

"Enough is enough, Mother," Libby's mom announced at dinner. "It is time you told us the truth. I'm not leaving this table until I have an explanation."

Libby's grandmother had busied herself with clearing the dishes, and she looked up from a plate of leftover carrots, a surprised expression on her face.

"Whatever do you mean, Gretchen?"

Mrs. Frye straightened her posture. "I mean, what has happened to Father? This is our second day here and I want to know what is going on. Father couldn't have just *disappeared* into thin air ... you had better tell us the truth. I mean it."

There was a long pause, and then Giselle turned around to face them, her eyes welling with tears. She sank into the nearest chair, buried her face in her hands, and began to sob.

"*Now*, Mother," frowned her mom.

"I did not want to ruin your Christmas," her grandmother whimpered, lifting her face for a moment. "That is all ... OOOHHHH!" She put her head back into her hands and proceeded to wail so loudly that Libby almost burst out laughing at the ridiculousness of it all. But she didn't, which took a tremendous amount of effort, because the harder she tried *not* to laugh, the more she could barely help it.

"Mother, please just tell us what is going on. H-have you been taking your medication?"

Giselle sniffed and peaked out between the fingers of her right hand. "Of course I have," she sniveled. "It is not that. It-it's your father," she paused for a few dramatic gasps. "H-he died. It was too late to tell you. I wanted to see Libby myself, y-you know a-and I th-thought we could a-at least all have a C-Christmas—I-I would have told you afterwards—OHHH ...." Her words dissolved into another round of loud sobbing.

For just a fraction of a second, the room was entirely still; even the cats froze in their tracks. And then, Libby accidentally dropped her fork.

"*WHAT?*" her mom roared, and Libby's dad sprang from the table, all the while glaring at her grandmother with an expression that Libby had never, ever seen on his face before.

"*You!*" he practically spat. "You deliberately lied to us! We were afraid something terrible was going to happen, but never dreamed you would stoop to this—" He broke off, and took a deep breath. "Actually, if I am to be honest, I suppose there is nothing you *wouldn't* stoop to!"

"I wanted to see Libby, too, you know. It wasn't just him!"

Mrs. Frye grunted in disgust. "Mother, you act as if you are some innocent, estranged, unappreciated, cast-off relative. After *everything*—and now—this!" Her eyes flashed and welled with tears at the same time. "We had his word—*your* word—that things were different, and now, well, I can't believe it! Father! Where-where is he buried? And, vhat … what did he die from? And when? How could you not *tell* me?" A tear slipped down her cheek as she looked miserably at her mother who still sat at the kitchen table, wringing a dishtowel in her pudgy hands.

"I had such plans for tonight—a wonderful holiday time together," Giselle whimpered, and then before anyone could say anything else, she flung herself from her chair and ran out of the kitchen, wailing loudly all the way down the hall.

"Unbelievable," Libby's dad muttered as a bedroom door slammed shut.

"Poor Father," her mom said quietly. "I would have come sooner if I had known. I never even said goodbye."

Libby stared from one to the other, not knowing what to think or say or even what to feel. She was so confused. She'd just found out that she *had* a grandfather, and now, he was gone, before she'd even had a chance to meet him, and no one seemed inclined to explain to her what in the world was going on.

"It's not your fault, Gretchen," her dad was saying. "Your mother—she did this on purpose. She—"

"Let's get out of here, Peter! Tomorrow morning. W-we'll go to town and find somewhere to stay until our flight. Who knows? We might even stay with Wolfgang."

"If that is what you want, Gretchen, of course," replied her dad, but her mom just looked even more miserable than before, her wide, violet eyes brimming with tears. She turned away and stumbled toward their room. Libby watched after her, feeling increasingly confused.

"Grandfather's dead," she murmured, and there was a part of her that had hoped the sound of it would somehow help make sense of things. But it didn't. It just made it more depressing.

"I'm so sorry, Libby," said her dad, patting her head the way he used to when she was little and would be upset over something. "I wish you could have met him, too."

"Just like that," she said dazedly. "Gone. And none of this makes any sense."

"No, it doesn't," he agreed, his voice strangely reserved; he took her hand and began walking toward their room.

Libby followed beside him, the sound of her mother's quiet sobs meeting her grandmother's louder ones in the damp hallway, and she shivered, suddenly feeling as if the chill had fingers that were trying to grab at her, trying to pull her down somewhere deep and dark, and she wished she could get out of this place; she wished she could be at Uncle Frank's house instead, where things were fun and light and brilliantly bizarre. She wondered what Uncle Frank was doing right now: if he was in the middle of inventing some new application for his mobile unit, or if he was outside with Buttercup, grumbling about having to put a leash on a goose ....

But Libby couldn't have known that Uncle Frank's house was far from cheerful at the moment, because he was having a crisis of his own, and it was definitely annoying enough to put him in a foul temper.

After all, Uncle Frank was not pleased with Esmerelda's progress, not in the least. He had such hopes for her, but her cognitive abilities had not increased at his anticipated rate, despite Uncle Frank's thought-simulation device installed days ago. Instead of the device acting as Uncle Frank had planned, it had triggered Esmerelda's more unstable reactions— transforming her initial self-preservation instincts into more human and volatile emotions. As a result, Esmerelda developed into an increasingly temperamental robot, taking any criticism or correction of Uncle Frank's as the deepest imaginable insult.

Today, Esmerelda apparently felt that Uncle Frank had been unreasonable when she had failed to properly break his eggs for breakfast. How was *she* supposed to know that he had wanted them to be cooked in a pan? Logically, it was a far more efficient way to break eggs by throwing them against the wall ….

Uncle Frank's reaction at seeing his kitchen oozing with sticky egg matter was not what Esmerelda had expected. If she could have cried, she would have. But being a robot, she could only simulate indignation, and so off she went, tearing about the house in a robotic frenzy, doing her best to indicate emotional injury at Uncle Frank's lack of appreciation toward her efforts.

Uncle Frank was in a roaring mood as he slung his mobile unit about the house, desperately trying to catch up with a belligerent robot. "Come here, Esmerelda! I just need you to stand still for one second!"

"Stand-still-question-mark," Esmerelda called in her most peevish voice that, despite her efforts, only sounded like a robot speaking slightly faster that normal. "What-does-stand-still-mean-question-mark. Does-it-mean-anything-like-break-some-eggs-for-breakfast-question-mark."

Uncle Frank's face burned purple with frustration as his mobile unit whined under its strain. It was his third time around the ground floor of his house—and the second time in and out of the front door—chasing after a robot who, by this time, had managed to successfully knock over or crush practically every piece of furniture that lay in its way. He was so intent on chasing down Esmerelda, that he didn't notice the white blur of a goose waddling stealthily through the living room.

"ESMERELDA!" he bellowed. "If you do not stop this second, I will *never* give you a single other upgrade!"

Esmerelda stopped instantly, her metal frame wavering a bit from the sudden change of motion. "I-like-upgrades."

Uncle Frank's eyes widened. "Yes, I know," he said, wheeling over to her. Reaching gently behind her head, he opened a small metal flap that swung sideways on a hinge. With a tiny screwdriver, Uncle Frank turned a small, shiny pin. "Goodness knows, after today, you need more than one!" he added, annoyed, as he continued to adjust something at the back of her head. "Just look at this place!"

"Well-I-," but before Esmerelda could finish her sentence, Uncle Frank turned the pin again and the little robot instantly went limp.

Uncle Frank sighed with relief—the emergency sleep mode actually worked! Now, he just had to get her back up to the shop. He definitely needed to do some more work on her before she did any more damage. With this kind of temper, she was a menace to society. *Society* of course encompassing a very small microcosm, indeed. Now that his nephew's family had left for a week, Uncle Frank was completely alone. Completely alone, that is, except for ....

"Buttercup!" Uncle Frank yelped, rushing toward the front door that was still open from chasing after Esmerelda.

What if ....

With a groan, Uncle Frank looked up to see a determined looking goose with a conspicuous purple berry necklace flying out the door and into the grey sky.

"Buttercup, come back!" Uncle Frank cried after him, but Buttercup only returned his plea with a friendly honk.

Uncle Frank sat helplessly in his mobile unit, watching as Buttercup's white and purple form grew smaller and smaller in the distance. Soon, he was nothing but a speck in the vast, grey sky.

6

THE HIDDEN STAIRCASE

Sunlight streamed through the cracks of the shuttered window as Libby awoke and stretched on her mattress. Yesterday's events came flooding into her memory. She rubbed her eyes, propped herself up on her elbow, and looked around the room. Her mom and dad stood by the window, speaking in low voices. Hearing Libby's movements, they stopped their whispering and smiled down at her.

"Good morning, Sassafras," said her mom. Her face was still puffy from crying the night before, but otherwise, she looked in considerably better spirits. "Go ahead and get dressed, and then we will leave straight away for Hanau."

Libby grinned in relief, jumped up and ran into the bathroom. She showered and dressed as quickly as she could, not wanting to spend any more time in this place than she had to. It was far too depressing. When she came back to the room, her parents had packed all of the bags and had put on their coats.

"Now, we are just going to stay calm, and tell your grandmother goodbye. No arguments. We'll probably have to walk all the way to town because she'll have disconnected the phone or something to keep us from calling a taxi, so you had better bundle up," she instructed, wrapping a thick scarf around Libby's neck and pulling a cap over her head. "Here's your coat, Libby, go ahead and put it on."

Libby surprised herself by doing exactly as she was told, even suffering the scratchy, woolen scarf without complaint. Her mother surveyed her, pulling wool mittens onto each of her hands, then nodded in approval.

She took a deep breath, grabbed one of the bags and marched down the hallway. Libby followed behind her father, feeling ridiculous in the unfamiliar winter garb. It was hard to walk without tottering from side to side like a drunken penguin.

"Frohes Fest," chirped Libby's grandmother as soon as they reached the kitchen. "Merry Christmas!"

"Oh, my goodness," said Libby, blinking in disbelief, because her grandmother was standing before them, dressed to the festive nines in a red sweater, bright green leggings, and a white apron with green embroidered pine trees. A red silk ribbon with bells was tied around her head.

"Mother!" gasped Mrs. Frye.

Giselle took a breath and stepped cautiously towards them.

"I know things didn't go so well yesterday, and that I was wrong to do what I did. For that, I am sorry."

Libby's parents looked at each other, dumbfounded.

"I really am," she continued cheerfully. "What I did was inconsiderate and unforgivable."

"But that doesn't change things, you apologizing, Mother. We're still leaving," Mrs. Frye finally managed.

Giselle patiently held up her hand. "I know, I know," she said calmly. "I deserve it, I certainly do. And you are free to go—I'll even call a cab for you."

Libby's parents exchanged more blank looks.

"But," continued Giselle, "I have one favor to ask."

Libby's dad sighed.

"All I want is for us to have breakfast together before you go," her grandmother continued, staring dejectedly at the freshly baked strudel steaming on the kitchen counter. "That's all. Since we won't be together for Christmas morning, let's at least part on a happier note. After all, it is Christmas Eve!"

Libby's mom groaned, dropped her bag and walked over to the table. "Fine, Mother, breakfast it is—if it is so important to you. But after that, we are going."

Giselle beamed. "Thank you, dear, thank you!"

Libby and her father slowly walked over to the table and sat down.

Giselle placed something on Libby's plate. "That one is just for you, Libby!"

"Um, thanks," said Libby, noticing that her name was spelled out with decorative, green sprinkles on top.

"And for the rest of us, I have baked a delicious, traditional strudel without the extra sweets that children so often expect," she cooed, throwing an indulgent glance at Libby, who was wrinkling her nose. "Although I must say, I am not very hungry, as I have been sampling things all morning … but if you two don't have any, it will hurt my feelings terribly. Really, I must insist!" she trilled brightly, cutting the pastry into generous portions, and placing a large piece on each of Libby's parents' plates.

"Merry Christmas!" she beamed.

Libby's dad looked around the table, his expression uneasy. "Yes. Merry Christmas," he managed.

"Cheers," said her mom who, most uncharacteristically, picked up the strudel with both hands and practically inhaled it. In under three minutes, she stood up and brushed the crumbs from her blouse onto her empty plate. Libby stared at her mom in astonishment. "Thank you, Mother," she said, her voice still tight and unfeeling. "That was very good. Did you put a new spice in it? It tasted a bit different than I remember."

"Oh? Well, no, dear, I don't think there was anything new. Perhaps it has just been so long since you've had my cooking."

Her mom picked a sticky crumb from her sleeve. "Yes, perhaps. Now, will you please call us a taxi?"

Libby gulped at her mom's rudeness and glanced uneasily back at her grandmother, half expecting to see another drama like last night, but instead, her grandmother merely nodded and walked over to the telephone, smiling serenely all the way. Libby listened to the foreign words being spoken and, within two minutes, her grandmother returned to the table. "They said it would take about fifteen minutes to get here."

"That's fine. Thank you, Mother."

Libby's dad took a final gulp of coffee and stood up from the table. "Thank you, Giselle," he said, his voice much gentler than before, and before he could offer to help, she had snatched his plate and began clearing the others off the table.

"My pleasure," she answered quickly. "Now, why don't the three of you just relax in the living room? I really must insist."

"Well, all right. I suddenly do feel sleepy ...." Her dad trailed off with a yawn, and he stumbled over to the living room couch.

Libby's mom yawned, too. "Must be all the jetlag," she mumbled, walking in a slight zigzag after him. "Fifteen minutes ...."

"You guys are getting old!" laughed Libby. "I don't feel a bit tired!"

But her mom only smiled wanly in response as she flopped onto the couch. Her eyes fluttered closed, and within seconds, she was fast asleep. Surprised, Libby turned to her father, who was looking goofily about him in a vacant sort of way.

"Dad, are you alright?"

"Oh! Libby! Hello! Why, of course ... jetlag ...." And before he could utter another word, he slumped over her mom, and began snoring loudly.

Her grandmother finished clearing the table and then walked over to the door. "The taxi should be coming soon," she called, looking out of the glass pane. "Better wake up your parents, Libby."

But Libby was already shaking them, first her mother, then her father, calling their names and pushing them with all of her strength. "Mom! Dad! Get up!" she shouted, but they only slumped further over after each push. "Mom! Dad! Get up! Please, get up! GRANDMOTHER!"

"What, dear? No need to shout!"

"They won't wake up!" cried Libby, shaking them both furiously. "I can't wake them up!"

Her grandmother stared at them for a few seconds, as if disbelieving it herself. Finally, she said, "We-we have to get them to the hospital … we'll use the taxi …." And just then, the sound of an engine jerked Libby to attention. She jumped up and ran to the front door as a large, grey van pulled into the yard.

"That doesn't look like a taxi."

The driver's side opened and a tall woman stepped out. Libby's eyes widened at the sight of her, for she was a very imposing-looking taxi driver, with a stern, but regal—almost beautiful—face, long, grey skirts, a fitted black velvet jacket and long, dark hair that was swept up into a twist at the top of her head. It was difficult to tell how old the woman was, for her hair was a mixture of black and grey, and her posture was a bit stooped, like someone late in years—maybe even seventy or so, but when the woman looked at Libby, her eyes sparked with a brilliant green that made everything about her seem younger.

CHAPTER 6

The woman strode with long, brisk steps toward the house and through the front door, now speaking loudly to her grandmother in German. Libby ran after her, but as soon as she reached the kitchen, the woman was turning around again.

"She's going to get the stretchers," murmured her grandmother, her voice trembling slightly.

"*Stretchers?*" wailed Libby. "Why does a taxi driver have *stretchers?*" But the stranger ignored her and swished out of the kitchen.

"Don't make her mad," whispered her grandmother in obvious agitation. "She's practically the only driver working on Christmas Eve!"

Libby gulped back her panic and ran after the woman again, halting in surprise as the woman strolled to the rear of the van and opened up the back doors. And then, if this wasn't already the strangest taxi Libby had ever seen, two men hopped out. The men must have been twins: they looked identical in every way, with black hair slicked straight back, very pale skin and strange, dark eyes that moved too quickly, so that their gaze almost felt inhuman. Nimbly, they pulled a stretcher from the back and scuttled toward the house.

"I often drive for the hospitals," announced a voice, and the sound of it made Libby jump straight into the air. She looked up to see the woman towering over her, her jewel-like eyes watching her intently.

"It is most fortunate for you that I am here," continued the woman coolly. "Your parents require my facilities, no? So please show my assistants the vay."

"The living room, Libby," whispered her grandmother.

"Oh. Over here," gulped Libby, suddenly realizing that she had been crying, and she wiped her eyes as she led the two strange men to the couch where her parents were still fast asleep.

The men dropped the stretcher and walked over to her dad, lifting him onto it and then scurrying him over to the van with a mechanical kind of efficiency. In a little over a minute, they were back with another stretcher and Libby watched helplessly as they lifted her mother and carried her away in the same manner. This time, Libby followed them—afraid to let them out of her sight—but as soon as they slipped her mother into the back of the van, the two men jumped into the back as well, slamming the doors shut before Libby could climb inside.

"Hey! Wait! Let me in!" Libby shouted, tugging uselessly on the locked handles. Her grandmother and the woman were talking loudly and, a second later, the woman walked over to the driver's door and opened it. "Wait!" Libby wailed, turning desperately to her grandmother. "Aren't we going too? I can't just leave them! Where are they going? Wh—"

"Children are not allowed," replied the woman.

Libby turned pale.

"But I have to go with them. I-I can't *leave* them!"

"Trust me, dear, this is not easy for me, either," said her grandmother, placing her hands over Libby's shoulders. "But what she says is true; the emergency rooms don't allow minors, so we'll have to wait here for the time being. She'll call us soon."

And with that, the woman nodded tersely, hopped into the driver's seat and took off with surprising speed.

It was a blur from there on out, but Libby recalled being led back into the house, her grandmother murmuring about hospital legalities and other things that only made Libby feel terrified, angry and even more confused. Four whole hours ticked by. And then, finally, the phone rang. Her grandmother quickly picked up the receiver, spoke a few words in German, and then listened as something was said on the other end. She nodded gravely, her face growing pale. She hung up the receiver.

"What?" gasped Libby. "What did they say?"

"It seems … that your parents have … passed."

"What-what do you mean by *passed?*"

Her grandmother didn't reply at first, but stumbled over to one of the kitchen cabinets instead. Her hands shook as she took a small, plastic bottle from the top shelf, pouring several little pink pills into her palm and popping them into her mouth.

"Died, dear," she whispered, staggering back to the table and sinking into one of the chairs opposite where Libby sat. "Some rare strain of food poisoning. Apparently it was the airplane food … already in their blood. Oh, my nerves …."

Libby stared in horror at her grandmother, too shocked to respond in any way. Her ears were ringing. The room seemed as if it were suddenly filling with a black fog, swirling and swirling before her eyes and her grandmother's face swirled right along with it. No, no, this couldn't happen.

She was breathing very quickly now with sharp, short breaths, but they were too fast and she couldn't get any air, but it couldn't be real, not her parents, not *here*. The blackness circled closer around her and she felt as if she were falling with her sharp, short breaths, slipping into the dizzying darkness, in out in out in out ….

Libby's eyes fluttered closed as she fainted, slumping over the kitchen table.

The sunlight twinkled through the shuttered windows, gleaming in slivers upon Libby's unconscious face. Her grandmother rose unsteadily from the table with a sob and staggered over to the other side of the kitchen. Somewhere in the shadows, a door creaked open and then, in the next moment, her grandmother was gone.

When Libby woke up, the room was dark; she couldn't tell if it was night or early morning, but in the next second, it didn't matter, because the memory of her parents came oozing back in.

An empty pit in her stomach seemed to open up and drag her inwards, and Libby moaned, wishing she had not awakened. She stayed still for several minutes, feeling frozen somehow so that, even in her despair, she also felt detached— almost numb, as if not able to completely take it in—and the numbness made it seem to her that nothing was real, nothing existed, and that she was floating in a big, black universe that would never end, and everything she had ever known before had only been a dream.

CHAPTER 6

In her odd state of mind, all she could do was look blankly about her, until slowly, her eyes adjusted to the darkness. A door to what she supposed was a pantry hung slightly ajar.

For no reason in particular, she got up from the table, the sensation of movement feeling strange to her, as if it didn't belong to a body that already felt dead, and she moved towards it, not really caring or curious, but just moving because that's what her brain had signaled for her to do. When she reached the pantry, she saw a narrow, wooden staircase inside. It didn't even surprise her.

She stepped trance-like through the opening, climbing the stairs until they ended at an open doorway that led to a dimly-lit attic.

She looked around indifferently, and then noticed with a sort of detached surprise that her grandmother was slumped in an over-stuffed chair just under the attic window, fast asleep, still clutching the orange bottle of medicine in one hand. Her head was rolled to one side, a trickle of saliva dangling from the corner of her mouth, and jiggling up and down as she snored loudly. But what really caught Libby's attention was her grandmother's lap, because sprawled across her knees was the forest green Grimm Brothers book, and at her feet, lay Libby's opened backpack.

Instinctively, Libby lurched toward her things, feeling indignant at discovering them in such a manner. She didn't understand it. And then she noticed other peculiar details about the room as well, such as the odd bits of paper tacked here and there like pieces of a puzzle, each piece a fragment of hand-drawn map, with notes she couldn't read, and a shelf to one side of the room with an official-looking folder resting on the surface.

Libby wandered over to it, and saw that it was a binder of sorts, with a dark blue hard cover, and with the name of some Frankfurt law firm in neat, silver letters on the bottom left corner. She lifted the cover and saw a short stack of papers underneath, grouped into two separate clips. The first group of papers—only three total—were all written in German, but then, to Libby's astonishment, underneath these, was a large envelope, stamped, dated two months earlier and addressed to her mother at their home in Baluhla! Libby could see that it had been opened; she removed the contents and, discovering that it was written in English, began to read.

Now, Libby had never read a will before, but it didn't take long before it became clear to her that this was exactly what she was doing, and to be more precise, that she was reading her late grandfather's will. And what it had to say really shocked her back to her senses. The papers dropped from her hands. The next thing she knew, she was running downstairs as fast as she could go, rooting through her bag at the same time for her walkie-talkie. She pressed the button just as she reached the kitchen.

"Ginny! Are you there?" Libby called, and she noticed that her hands were shaking. She released the button and waited a few seconds. The fuzzy static from the other end flowed through the speaker, and Libby could hardly believe it when she heard Ginny's voice.

"*Libby?*" Ginny replied anxiously. "Holy Macaroni! I-I didn't really think these things wou—"

"Ginny, listen to me," Libby cut in, trying her best to remain calm. "I-I don't have much time to talk, but I need you to reach Uncle Frank. Something terrible has happened. My parents—I don't know. Grandmother says they died!"

The sound of her saying it out loud, to someone outside in the real world, to her best friend, did something to her. It made it more real, more desperate.

"What are you *talking* about?" Ginny gasped.

Libby shook herself. "She said food poisoning," she barely managed, because her throat choked on the words. "Yesterday, I think, but I don't know if it's true, I can't believe it … she lied to us about Grandfather, too, and I don't know what's going on and now, I think I just found a will from him with our address, like it had been *mailed* but intercepted or something, and there's a letter from Grandfather with it that warns Mom not to come and it says he left a fortune and that there's a key hidden in that book we brought, and I've just found my stuff upstairs where my grandmother must have been looking for it … none of this makes sense!" she screamed into the radio, completely forgetting herself. "Something terrible is happening and I'm stuck here!" she sobbed. "I don't know about my parents; I don't even know where they are; I don't know what to *do!*"

Libby suddenly stopped, because the front door to the kitchen opened, and the tall woman from the taxi stepped through it, her eyes blazing with an expression Libby could not understand. And then, from behind her, she heard her grandmother's footsteps stumbling down the hidden stairway.

She opened her mouth to say something, but nothing came out, only an icy, cold wave of dread that washed over her and froze her to the spot.

"Libby! Libby, are you there?" Ginny called.

The emerald-eyed woman swept toward her and grabbed the walkie-talkie from Libby's grasp, knocking her bag and book to the floor in the process.

She dashed the radio to the ground, sending pieces of plastic scuttling across the floor. Static crackles streamed for a moment from the speaker, followed by a few intermittent blips before ending in silence. The sudden quiet cleared Libby's head and she realized that she was being pulled through the doorway.

"Where did you take my parents?" she gasped, struggling against the woman, but her grip was like a vise, and it was all Libby could do to stumble clumsily down the porch stairs after her.

The woman yanked Libby toward a large, black sedan waiting in the yard. The trunk door yawned opened. It took a moment for Libby to realize that she was actually being lifted, but by the time she started kicking, it was no use; her legs flailed in the air. She landed on her back inside the trunk as an object fell over her face. It was her red winter coat.

"Wait! Zelna, what are you doing?" wailed another voice, and as Libby scrambled up, she could just make out the top of her grandmother's white, curly hair as she came wobbling toward the car.

CHAPTER 6

"Get me out of here!" screamed Libby, struggling to climb out of the trunk, but the green-eyed woman called Zelna pushed her back down. "Help! Grandmother! Don't let her do this!"

"Stay out of it, Giselle," barked Zelna. "Remember vhat we agreed."

"Libby!" her grandmother called with genuine alarm, and then she wailed something in German as the trunk slammed shut.

Libby lay huddled inside the darkness, listening as her grandmother's screaming was met with calm, foreign words. She continued to kick and push at the trunk door, but it was useless. The sound of the engine sliced through their voices. Libby felt the wheels roll underneath her, increasing with speed, and soon, her grandmother's cries faded into the rumbles of the road.

7

FUGITIVE

Five thousand miles away, Ginny sat in her room, staring blankly at her walkie-talkie that had suddenly gone silent. It was half past midnight, but Ginny wasn't sleeping. It had been the worst day of her life, and it had started much, much earlier when Delbert and Ernestine Snookles got into a huge fight.

Ginny didn't know if it was the eggnog Delbert had spiked or simply the stress of the holiday season, but somebody must have done *something* to set it all off, and even though Ginny locked herself in her room while they screamed at each other, she couldn't help but overhear them. The more the Snookles screamed, the more ridiculous they got, and toward the end, Ginny heard Mr. Snookles blaming *her* of all people for his foul temper.

"We need to send that kid back to the home," he eventually declared. "I've been downright uneasy since she's been here, that's really what the problem is; I haven't felt myself."

Of course "the home" was none other than Brownsby County's Group Home for Foster Children, a place Ginny had been in and out of since she was three.

Libby knew the truth of course; Ginny had told her a month ago, but had sworn her to secrecy, and the truth was that the Snookles were no more her uncle and aunt than Santa Clause and whatever his wife's name was. Jessica, maybe? Or was it Maria?

Well, it didn't matter and normally, being sent back to the group home wouldn't either—after all, it had happened plenty of times before.

But this time, things were different. She *liked* it here. She had a friend, a real one. She didn't want to go away, because that would mean she'd be over an hour from Baluhla and she'd never get to see her best friend ….

Ginny had spent the rest of that evening pacing the floor of her room, worrying over what she could possibly do to convince the Snookles not to send her away, when her walkie-talkie had blared into life. Libby's voice had flooded out of it, saying things so strange that Ginny could barely comprehend them. And then, right when Libby's frantic words were starting to make some sense, the walkie-talkie fell silent. Ginny still stared down at the radio in her hands, her brain bouncing thoughts like a million rubber balls.

Dead? The Fryes? It couldn't be. She must have misunderstood, it was all so fast, and the radio had too much static … and then, Libby had said something about her grandfather ….

The ping-ponging of her thoughts froze.

Whatever was the matter, it was clear that Libby was in danger. She had to take a risk for once; she had to be brave and do whatever she could to save her friend. The Snookles would never help her, much less believe her, and besides, they were both probably too snockered on eggnog to be of any use.

"I can do this," Ginny whispered over the pounding of her heart. "She's counting on me and I have to do this; I can't wait until morning."

She stood up with purpose and swiftly packed her bag—the same small bag that had made trips between foster homes in the past—slipping in her walkie-talkie, a flashlight and a few changes of clothes. She knew exactly where she needed to go, and she didn't have a minute to lose. She opened her bedroom window. And then, for the first time in her life, Ginny broke the rules.

When Uncle Frank opened his front door that morning, no invention in the world could have prepared him for such a sight. Ginny was passed out on the porch, her walkie-talkie clutched in one hand, her bag somehow tangled in her shoelaces, and calmly sitting on the floor right beside her, was Esmerelda, apparently attempting some kind of woven masterpiece with Ginny's hair.

"Esmerelda, leave her alone!" Uncle Frank exclaimed in astonishment, and his voice jerked Ginny from her slumbers. She scrambled to a sitting position, looking rather bewildered, as though uncertain as to whether or not she was really awake.

"Is ... is she braiding my hair?"

"Ignore her," grunted Uncle Frank. "What I want to know is, what is the matter? How on earth did you even *get* here?"

It took Ginny a few more seconds to compose her thoughts, and then she looked around again.

"Where's Buttercup?"

Uncle Frank scowled. "Looking for Libby, I suppose. I'm sure he'll come back when he gets hungry enough—but I don't want to talk about Buttercup, Ginny. What's happened to *you?*"

Ginny looked into Uncle Frank's gruff face, trying to assess his mood.

"If I tell you," she began warily, "will you promise me that you won't send me right back to the Snookles, and that you'll hear me out, even if it sounds crazy?"

"Why wouldn't I?"

"Just promise me!"

"Okay ... I promise," grumbled Uncle Frank, who, as a general rule, absolutely hated to make promises of any sort. "Now what the heck is going on?"

And Ginny told him everything, including the part about the Snookles fight and how Delbert was going to send her back to the group home, if he had his way, and she thought that he definitely would.

She told him all about Libby's walkie-talkie call, how it

suddenly ended even though she knew Libby wasn't finished speaking, and how she'd decided to sneak out to tell him, and then she even told him about borrowing the neighbor's powder blue scooter to get here, but two miles before she'd reached his house, a wheel had broken off and she had to leave it by the side of the road, and she felt awful about it and really hoped she wouldn't get arrested for theft—on Christmas no less, which was sure to incur an additional penalty—but this last part just made her feel worse. At least Uncle Frank listened intently, which surprised her; he didn't interrupt once, and even more surprising, was the fact that she could tell by his drawn expression that he wasn't just listening, but that he actually believed her.

❋ ❋

An hour later, Ginny and Uncle Frank were still on the front porch, staring gloomily into the December sky.

Ginny huddled closer into the quilt Uncle Frank had brought her, shivering from a combination of fatigue and cold, but she didn't want to go inside, not until they had figured out what they were going to do, and besides, the chilly air helped her think. A small dot of an airplane moved in from the horizon, cutting soundlessly through the sky.

It was now seven o'clock on Christmas morning.

"So, should we contact the authorities or something?" prompted Ginny, who wasn't entirely sure who or what the "authorities" would be in this case.

Uncle Frank answered slowly, his eyes focused on the yard in front of him. "I'm not sure, Ginny. I'm trying to think it through. I don't have a phone, but I do have a HAM radio that I can fix up to call the sheriff ...."

"Great!" said Ginny. "Let's do it!"

Uncle Frank frowned.

"Yes, but the problem is, I'm nothing more than a crazy old man calling on a radio and you're a runaway ten-year-old foster kid who is claiming to have received a call from her best friend in Germany on a walkie-talkie."

Ginny pushed down the quilt and scowled.

"If they take it even somewhat seriously," Uncle Frank continued, "they'll go straight to the Snookles who, from all I have heard, will assure the police you are nothing short of an overly imaginative, meddling, silly little girl. Maybe even troubled, with issues that require professional help ...."

"I'm *not* troubled."

"*I* know you're not, but that's not the point."

"Go on."

"Well, we could try to radio the American Embassy, but I don't know the frequency for that, and even if I did, we would get the same response: an old man's paranoia and a little girl's word that she heard something from a walkie-talkie."

Ginny's shoulders slumped. "Doesn't instill a lot of confidence, does it?"

"'Fraid not," said Uncle Frank. "But I still plan to try. It all makes sense now," he muttered. "I saw the stone, but couldn't quite believe it ...."

"What stone?" asked Ginny, but her question was met with silence, and when she looked over at him again, it was evident that Uncle Frank was suddenly miles away. She'd seen him like this before, when he'd been thinking over a problem with Esmerelda, and she knew that it was no use trying to talk to him.

She sighed heavily and waited.

After a while, he turned to her. It almost looked as though he had been crying, but no tears were on his face, only something in his eyes that looked like anguish—like fear.

"You're sure she said those words?" he asked in a low, hoarse voice. "She said they were *dead?*"

Ginny swallowed hard and nodded. She still couldn't believe it herself. "This isn't right, Uncle Frank," she declared. "I mean, *food poisoning?* It just sounds so strange … and Libby sounded really scared!"

"I told them not to go; I begged Peter to listen to me," he whispered, holding his head in his hands so that his long fingers snaked in and out of his wiry hair, "but he said it was no use, that they'd argued and discussed it for weeks, and he'd never seen Gretchen so resolute before, almost as though someone else had made the decision for her …." The rumble of a plane overhead drowned out the rest of his words.

"But that's just the thing!" Ginny shouted over the noise. "You obviously knew something bad might happen, so what was it? What happened all those years ago?"

The rumbling dissolved into the distance.

"Libby's parents might already be dead," Ginny reminded

him. "If we have a chance of saving Libby at all, the truth needs to come out."

"The truth should have come out a long time ago," Uncle Frank replied wearily, "but even I don't know what happened. I've drawn conclusions where possible, that's all."

"What conclusions?"

Uncle Frank seemed to think this over for a moment.

"Alright, Ginny," he sighed. "It's not much, but here's what I know …."

Ginny nodded eagerly.

"Peter first met Gretchen when he was stationed in Hanau, Germany, with the Army," he began slowly. "He'd met her at a bakery downtown; there was some funny story associated with that, but I could never remember it correctly. It had something to do with a mutual friend of theirs named Wolfgang who owned the place; I think Gretchen must have apprenticed under him. Anyway, right when Peter's tour was over, he and Gretchen eloped. Apparently, her mother was extremely controlling, and so they'd kept their relationship a secret.

"After their wedding, when Gretchen and Peter returned to her home to collect her things, her mother grew furious when she discovered the truth. From what little Gretchen has told me, it sounds as if her mother actually tried to hold Gretchen captive, to keep her from moving out with Peter … and something more than that as well. Something much worse than I am able to understand—neither Gretchen nor Peter has ever spoken of it to me. I'm not sure what happened, but when I saw them after they'd arrived back here, Peter had a terrible wound, right below his shoulder. It looked as if someone had actually stabbed him," Uncle Frank concluded quietly.

"She *stabbed* Mr. Frye?" Ginny whispered. "She tried to *kill* him?"

Uncle Frank nodded again.

"Peter never told me, so I can only assume, but I know from the extent and location of his injury that it should have been lethal. I'm still amazed at how well it healed, but my boy's always had a solid constitution," he added proudly. "Poor Gretchen was just a complete mess, convinced that it was somehow all her fault—completely ridiculous, of course."

"And that's the last time she saw her parents?"

"And that's the last time she saw them. And whatever actually *did* happen, when Libby came along, Gretchen became extremely paranoid about her safety. She went to great lengths to hide their whereabouts from anyone in her past life; it was strange, and I never understood it."

Another roar blasted upon them. Clouds of exhaust billowed in the sky as Uncle Frank and Ginny sat on the front porch, stunned, their ears reverberating from the loud engine sounds. The belly of a plane swooped over their heads, barely clearing Uncle Frank's house. Ginny hopped out of her chair and ran to the porch steps, craning her neck to see the plane as it circled in the sky, now heading away from them.

She hobbled back to her chair and looked at Uncle Frank in amazement. "Can you believe that? I've never seen one fly that close before! We could've been killed!"

Uncle Frank nodded, a funny expression filling his face.

Ginny straightened in her chair and cleared her throat. "So anyway, back to Libby's parents ...." But she was cut off once more by the blare of the plane's engine. This time, the plane skimmed over the tips of the surrounding trees, the engine rumbling louder and louder as the plane grew closer and closer. Ginny watched with widening eyes.

"Uh oh."

The plane continued to sink through the sky, its wheels unfolding from its belly like rounded talons as it drew nearer, towards the vast field in front of Uncle Frank's house. Seconds later, the wheels hit the dry ground, sending up billows of dust along with the blasting sounds of the engine.

The roaring continued as the plane scuttled across the wide lawn, toward the porch where Ginny and Uncle Frank sat riveted to their respective seats. And then, the plane began to slow down, moving slower across the field, leaving in its wake a giant cloud of smoke, dust and dried leaves before finally rolling to a stop. As the haze cleared, the twosome blinked and, as if practicing a coordinated pantomime, they rubbed their eyes and blinked again.

"What the—" started Uncle Frank.

"Holy Macaroni!" gulped Ginny.

Because there, right smack in the middle of Uncle Frank's front yard, was the most unlikely sight that either would have expected to encounter while sitting on a porch that Christmas morning.

And it wasn't any ordinary airplane, either. From what

Ginny could determine, it was a very *old* plane. And painted below its nose, circling out to surround the lower sides of the cockpit, spread a menacing, toothy mouth that opened most disconcertingly in their general direction.

"Is that a shark's mouth?" squeaked Ginny.

"Well, if hell hasn't frozen over," said Uncle Frank.

Ginny's eyes were glued to the aberration. "What *is* that?" she whispered.

"That … is a P-40."

"What's a P-40?"

"An Army Air Corps fighter plane from before World War Two," answered Uncle Frank, his eyes fixed on the plane as the cockpit popped open. "I used to fly one."

From behind the other side of the plane, a figure descended, hobbled around the shark's mouth and through the settling dust toward the wide-eyed pair, who sat huddled under their blankets.

Ginny squinted at the approaching figure. It was a man. An elderly man, she thought, wearing a leather helmet, goggles, a leather jacket and … a skirt? Ginny blinked and stared at the figure. Sure enough, from the waist down, the pilot approached with confident steps, shoeless and barelegged, wearing nothing but a loose, cotton cloth that looked like a hospital gown billowing in the breeze. Ginny glanced nervously at Uncle Frank.

His face had gone from awe, to confusion, to uncertainty and now, Ginny wasn't sure, but it almost looked like anger. Uncle Frank peeled the blankets from him, his eyes never

CHAPTER 7

leaving the approaching figure. He reached his hands down and pushed himself up inside his mobile unit so that he now sat tall and rigid, his chin thrust forward defiantly.

The pilot's bowlegged march continued until he had reached the bottom of the front porch steps. He halted, hands on his hips, legs spread apart and surveyed Uncle Frank with a withering stare.

"Now will somebody mind telling me," he bellowed, "what in *tarnation* is going on?"

8

FLYING TIGERS

"Well!" Uncle Frank exclaimed with unmistakable distaste.

"You know this man?" whispered Ginny.

"Darn skippy," the pilot retorted, his face screwed up irritably. "Sal McCool, the one and only, at your service. But I didn't leave my luxury hotel room for you to just sit there and admire my physical beauty. Where's the emergency? The life-threatening danger? All I see is an old fart sitting in a wheelchair with a ratty little girl."

Ginny was too shocked to respond, much less realize that she was being insulted.

"Oh, stuff it, Sal," said Uncle Frank wearily. "You haven't changed a bit, have you?"

"More than I can say 'bout you, old man."

"Old man, eh?" snapped Uncle Frank. "I'm not the one wearing a hospital gown. Mister-Luxury-Hotel-Room, my foot!"

Sal's eyes flashed, and much to Ginny's astonishment, Sal McCool began hopping around on his bare feet, doing a jig of sorts.

"Your foot? Ha! You don't have one to stand on, much less a leg," he cackled gleefully as he danced on the dirt ground. "Ha-ha! Bet you wish you had half of my energy!"

Uncle Frank rolled his eyes and held up a hand in appeasement. "Okay, Sal, we get it. You're in tiptop shape and I'm a pathetic, crippled old miser. Fine. You win."

Sal stopped his jig and stood still. His grin disappeared as he eyed Uncle Frank shrewdly. "Speaking of your incapacitated self, what is going on here? I got the summons."

Uncle Frank's eyes lit up. "The stone? Of course!"

Sal let out a loud, disgusted grunt. "Maybe it's 'of course' to you, but it sure ain't to me. Do you know how much trouble I had to go through to get here? I've flown all the way from El Paso. Had to sneak out of my stupid care—, er— hotel room, not to mention breaking and entering into an aviation museum. My good for nothing son's kept my plane there, ever since they forced me to retire my membership from the Confederate Air Force, stupid bunch of sissies. Best pilot in the Confederacy, I was. Taught the lot of 'em. That's gratitude for ya. I suppose I should be thankful that my plane's kept somewhere with an airfield, but I know it's only because he rents it out, that little—"

Sal looked up to see Uncle Frank and Ginny staring at him. He blushed and kicked a stone on the ground, apparently forgetting that he didn't have on any shoes. Sal winced and then glared back at them. "Well, anyway, I got here. And what do I find? *Not* an emergency, that much is clear."

"Ginny," Uncle Frank said, his eyes never leaving Sal's face, "allow me to introduce to you Salvador McCool. My old wing man from my Flying Tiger days and the only individual I know who is completely lacking amygdalae."

A confused look flickered in Sal's eyes.

"What's a Flying Tiger?" asked Ginny.

Uncle Frank cleared his throat. "I'll explain it all to you someday. Important you know your U.S. history, anyhow. They don't teach you youngsters anything worth knowing in school nowadays, do they?"

"Well, I'm only in fifth grade."

"Granted," said Uncle Frank. "But you're never too young to learn what our country has done for the life we all live now."

"Darned tootin'," chimed in Sal.

Uncle Frank frowned, evidently unsure how to feel about their agreement on a topic. "Anyway," he continued, "for the sake of clarity and reference, I'll merely tell you that, years and years ago, we had a ... falling out, I guess you could say."

"Over a darn woman!"

Uncle Frank bristled. "Sophia was no *darn woman*. She was …."

"Whatever," snapped Sal. "What you are trying to convey to your snot-nosed granddaughter here, is that we had a falling out."

"This is not my granddaughter. And Ginny is not snot-nosed."

"Thank you," said Ginny.

"In fact," Uncle Frank continued angrily, "I've never married, because *you* stole the only woman I ever loved. Then, in typical Sal fashion, you up and got yourself captured, *and then* I got shot in the back for rescuing your sorry, corpse of a soul, which, coincidently, is the whole reason why I'm in this 'wheelchair' as you put it!"

"Oh, cool it! It's why I'm here, isn't it? To pay off my debt to you? Never could let it go, could you?"

"Gentlemen!" Ginny yelled, surprising herself with her new-found assertiveness, but she was discovering that desperation makes a person do all sorts of things normally out of character. She wiggled out of her chair and stood on the porch between them, pausing for a moment to collect her thoughts, and then she said:

"Obviously, there is quite a history between you two, but since you can't speak to each other without fighting, please allow the *snot-nosed, ratty little girl* to fill you in."

Uncle Frank took a deep breath and Sal rolled his eyes. Ginny glared between them both.

"Now, I don't know what this 'summons' or 'stone' is about, but I can tell you what the emergency is, since that seems to be so important to you." She looked at Sal, who seemed to relax his stance. "My best friend, and Uncle Frank's grandniece, is in grave danger. She and her parents flew to Germany a few days ago and during that time, something terrible has happened to them …."

Ginny proceeded to relay the sequence of events that led up to their gathering, and Sal stood at full attention, paying no mind to the chilly draft that blew beneath his loose, cotton gown. When Ginny had finished, Sal shifted his weight and looked at Uncle Frank.

"Hanau, huh?"

Uncle Frank had his head buried in his hands. He nodded slightly.

"Flew a P-51 into that area after the Flying Tigers, you know, escorting bombers out of England."

Uncle Frank dropped his hands and looked at Sal with disgust. "Now, why would I care about that, McCool? We've just finished telling you that my nephew and his wife have been reported dead, and that my grandniece is in danger, and here you are, bragging about your war stories!"

Sal cleared his throat and looked at his bare feet. "And the stone?"

"I gave the third one to Libby."

"You've still got the other?"

Uncle Frank nodded.

"I want to see it."

"I've got it here."

Sal hobbled up the stairs toward Uncle Frank, passing Ginny with a grunt.

"Goodness!" she squeaked, turning wide-eyed to Uncle Frank.

Sal jerked a thumb towards her. "What's the matter with that girl?"

"Y-you don't have any underpants on!"

Uncle Frank followed Ginny's nervous glance and then snickered. "Sal, you are literally showing your backside, courtesy of your luxury-hotel-room gown. But at least you're consistent—exposing your true self, as it were."

Sal craned his neck around, grabbing the hem of his hospital gown and pulling it away as he struggled to see his posterior. Ginny groaned and covered her eyes with both hands, her ears now burning bright pink. "Just go put something on, *please!*"

"Inside Sal," barked Uncle Frank. "Go straight past the stairs and through the kitchen. You'll find a laundry room with a pair of pants in the dryer. For Pete's sake, put them on."

Sal sniffed and marched through the front door without another word.

Ginny's ears slowly returned to normal as she turned to face Uncle Frank. He threw her an apologetic glance and then opened up a box that he had taken from his jacket pocket, removing a thin material from the top. She watched as he pulled out a silver-colored chain, followed by a dangling, figure-eight shaped stone that glowed with a blue, pulsating beauty. It appeared to float upwards in the air, its light blazing and swirling from the inside as though the stone were made of liquid.

Ginny's mouth dropped open and she scrambled over to get a closer look. For a moment, both Uncle Frank and Ginny stared wordlessly at the glowing, swirling amulet.

"What *is* that?" she finally said.

"It's the stone, genius," muttered Sal, emerging through the front door. He had on trousers that were a good four inches too long for him and a pair of Uncle Frank's socks. Sal's left big toe stuck through a hole.

Ginny ignored him and looked at Uncle Frank.

"Well, it's a long story, Ginny, but it, like our cantankerous visitor, is from my Flying Tiger days," Uncle Frank nodded his head toward Sal's parked plane. "Sal and I flew planes like that one as part of the American Volunteer Group, before the United States had entered World War Two. To make a long story short, we, along with other Flying Tigers, flew out of Burma and China to fight the Japanese. We had a ground crewman named Lam, who helped maintain our aircraft whenever we landed between missions. He was an unusual fellow … grew up all over the place, fluent in at least ten languages, part Chinese, part Indian and Persian … maybe some Japanese, too, I can't remember. Anyway, in the event we were ever shot down, Lam gave Sal and me each a stone necklace." He held the glowing stone up so that it dangled loosely from its chain.

"But, there are three …."

"Lam had the third one. He claimed they were carved from an ancient rock hidden deep within the Himalayas. Part of his ancestry could be traced from there, and the amulets had been passed down in Lam's family from generation to generation. Lam was the last of his line to have them—his entire family had been killed off two years before."

Ginny stared, wide eyed, at the stone. She reached out a trembling hand and touched it. It felt cool and smooth. She looked up again at Uncle Frank, eager for him to continue.

"Well?"

"According to folklore, the stone contains magical qualities. The heart of the stone was carved into three separate amulets, one of which you're currently looking at. The chain and the binding around the amulet are actually made of titanium, strong enough to hold the stone when it is activated. When one of these is carried by a person, all others with a pendant carved from the same stone will know if they are in danger. It would glow, like this one."

Ginny sucked in her breath and stared again at the amulet, barely able to acknowledge what she was hearing. Magical stones? From the Himalayas? It was hard to believe, but then again, there was a World War Two plane with a shark's mouth parked in the yard, and she was talking to a ninety-plus-year-old man sitting in a hover-craft-like mobile unit, who, incidentally, had been in a bad mood ever since his invented robot had malfunctioned.

After all, she reasoned, anything was possible.

"So that means …."

Uncle Frank nodded. "Yes, Ginny. The glowing stone means that Libby is in danger. When Sal saw *his* stone glowing, he thought it was because *I* was in danger. He seems to believe he has a debt to repay me, and that being the case, he flew here to finally be free of his obligation."

Sal threw Uncle Frank a nasty look and then glared at his plane. "Ungrateful," he said under his breath, but loud enough for Uncle Frank to hear. "I said I would return the favor someday. You're just wanting to die the martyr is all."

Ginny shook her head, looking back and forth between the stone, Uncle Frank and Sal. "But then, why did you have *two* stones?"

Uncle Frank's warm eyes glowed distantly, his mind running over memories long stored away. "It happened right after Pearl Harbor; there was an ambush," he said slowly. "We were separated. With the help of the stone, I found Lam, but it was too late ... his last words were to take his necklace, and to give it to someone whom I treasured beyond all else." Ginny held her breath as she watched Uncle Frank, his expression still far, far way. And then abruptly, he shook himself, sniffed, and glanced over at Sal. "I found Sal two days later, and ... we narrowly escaped."

The front porch fell silent. The winter air hung, as if suspended in time, over the small group.

"That's when you were shot in the back?" guessed Ginny.

Sal turned to her with an annoyed smirk. "Regular Sherlock Holmes, aren't you?"

Ginny tried to ignore him.

"Yes, that's how dear old Frankie-boy here got shot," grunted Sal, throwing a gnawed piece of dried grass on the ground.

Silence fell again as Sal stared sulkily into the distance. Uncle Frank looked down at his necklace, with Ginny following his gaze. "You said, the stone helped you find Lam and Sal?" she asked quietly.

"Oh," Uncle Frank jerked, as if he were being tugged back into the present. "Yes—er, the stone, when worn and when in close enough proximity, it pulls toward the one in jeopardy. The closer you get, the stronger the pull. A kind of compass, really."

"Wow," Ginny whispered. "So now, it's not pulling, 'cause Libby's the one in danger?"

"Yes," murmured Uncle Frank. "She's too far away."

The group fell silent again, only to be broken by Sal's mutterings:

"I'll be stuck with this guilt my whole life. Over sixty years of waiting, and all I wanted was to repay my debt to the old cuss and die honorably."

"You can still pay off your debt, Sal," came a small, high-pitched voice.

Alarmed, Uncle Frank stopped staring at his necklace and looked at Ginny.

"That's right, Sal," she said. "You can fly *me* to Germany."

"What?" said Sal.

"*WHAT?*" croaked Uncle Frank.

"I said, Sal can fly me to Germany. *I'll* find Libby, and Sal can finally fulfill his obligation to *you.*"

"You're nuts," said Sal.

"I think that midnight run has affected your mind, little girl," said Uncle Frank.

Ginny stiffened and crossed her arms.

"Look," she said in the kind of voice one uses to talk to difficult, spoiled children. "I'm the only one who can help Libby. Uncle Frank, you certainly can't go. You're restricted to the abilities of your mobile unit."

"Now wait just a minute!"

But Ginny held up a hand.

"I don't mean that insultingly. We both know you'd already be on a plane over there if you could. But you can't. Besides the fact that you're, er, old, and, um, disabled, you've got your heart problem."

Sal snickered.

"Libby told me," continued Ginny, as she turned and looked him squarely in the eyes. "And don't try to deny it. If you were to get on that plane—or any plane—you wouldn't even make it to the Atlantic before you'd have to land somewhere near a hospital. And you know it."

Uncle Frank started to say something in protest but, deciding against it, closed his mouth and looked sullenly at the chubby girl standing before him.

"It's not a bad plan," Ginny continued excitedly, and the idea was coming to her so fast that she couldn't have possibly realized what she was suggesting. "Come to think of it, it's our only option. We already know that we can't get any authorities to help—they'd never take us seriously. But with the help of Sal's necklace, we can track her down, can't we, Sal?"

"It's impossible, anyway," cut in Uncle Frank before Sal could answer. "The P-40 is a single seater. There's no room for another person, not even a delusional, headstrong, runaway ten-year-old girl."

"Well, if you're just going to insult me, then you left out fat."

"Actually," Sal was saying, "remember the TP-40's? They were the exact same model, just with a second seat in the fuselage for training purposes ...."

"Shut up, McCool," snarled Uncle Frank.

"I'm just saying," bristled Sal, "theoretically speaking, it *is* possible to modify the plane. Just install another seat behind mine and a window hatch. I've heard of it being done before, and if it can be done, well, frankly, Frank, you're just the man to do it."

"He could do that in his sleep!" agreed Ginny, seizing the opportunity. "And it's not like he doesn't have the tools and materials!"

Sal frowned. "I was just speaking hypothetically, kid."

"Ginny, you're in *fifth grade*," Uncle Frank cut in.

Ginny blinked, taking a second to collect her thoughts, because she knew that what she said next—if she were very lucky and very careful—just might make a difference. "That's true," she replied, watching Uncle Frank closely, "but you've always said that we shouldn't allow ourselves to be defined by age or life circumstance."

Uncle Frank frowned and opened his mouth.

"And it's also true that, as a general rule, I'm a complete wimp," she continued before he could respond. "Libby's always been the brave one. But that's just it: I've been afraid my whole life of everything; I've followed all the rules and never acted out and never even had the guts to stand up for myself, and what for? To be bullied and shuffled between foster homes and schools and towns like an unwanted pet?

Libby is the first person to be my friend, to *believe* in me, Uncle Frank, and Mr. and Mrs. Frye, well, they've made me feel like family. I've never had that before, and now, Libby needs *my* help."

"But Ginny, this is ridiculous! There has got to be another way!"

Ginny shook her head, her expression pleading. "Like what? I know I can do this! I've got nothing to lose. Literally. The Snookles are going to send me away if I stay here. Besides, Sal will be with me, I mean, if he's serious about paying off that debt, so it's not like I'll be all alone."

Uncle Frank and Sal exchanged incredulous glances.

"C'mon, Uncle Frank," coaxed Ginny. "It's our only choice … you *do* want to help Libby, don't you?"

"Of course I do!"

"And Mr. and Mrs. Frye … we don't know what's happened, I mean, what she said … it just doesn't sound right."

Uncle Frank slumped in his mobile unit, shaking his head back and forth. Sal sat on the porch step, looking between Ginny and Uncle Frank. A smile crept across his puckered face.

"Ginny, you can't go to Germany," declared Uncle Frank. "And as for being sent away, that's preposterous. You can stay here with me, of course."

Ginny laughed; it sounded sharp and bitter. "Don't you think the Snookles will report that I've run away? Who do you think will be the first person Social Services will look toward, after finding the Fryes gone? *You.* There's no way they'd let me stay with a crazy, old man in a run-down mansion in the middle of the woods. No offense."

"She's right, you know."

"You stay out of this, McCool. You've caused enough problems for me."

"Here we go again!"

"Look," Ginny said, her voice full of conviction. "It's a good plan and our only plan. Libby needs help. Libby's parents are either dead or at the very least, in grave danger. We are *alone* in this. No one else can help us. Don't you understand that?" She looked at Uncle Frank, her eyes burning with a sense of purpose.

"I'll take my walkie-talkie, and I can communicate with you regularly if you can get another one to share my frequency," she said, her gaze still focused directly on Uncle Frank. "I'll find her—I know I can. Maybe I'm not related to them, but ... they're the closest thing to being my family, too, you know," she finished quietly.

Uncle Frank sighed, his shoulders slumping. "Their return flight isn't until tomorrow. If they're not here by the evening, then I'll know for sure," he whispered.

Ginny nodded excitedly, too elated by her success to be astonished that Uncle Frank was actually considering her proposal. "That's right. So, we can work on the plane today and if they're not back by tomorrow, Sal and I can leave the next morning. Don't worry—I'm used to going to strange places," she continued, increasingly encouraged by his silence. "I'll be fine. It's Libby we need to worry about."

Uncle Frank sank his head into his hands. "I can't believe I'm agreeing to this, but I don't see another option. If McCool's willing …."

"And-and the plane?" pressed Ginny. "Can you help with that?"

"I think so," he replied, sounding defeated. "I don't think I can modify it in my sleep, but I bet I could get it done within a day. But I'm only allowing this if Sal agrees to stay with you. I can fix up the HAM so that it can communicate both with your walkie-talkie and the plane's radio, so we can keep contact on the ground and in the air."

Ginny beamed. "Well, Sal?" she squeaked, her voice barely audible. "What do you say? Are you ready to pay off that debt?"

Slowly, Sal rose from his seat on the stairs and unzipped the breast pocket of his leather jacket, pulling out a battered, travel-worn map. Crouching on the porch, he spread the map upon the floor, the faded outlines of oceans and continents smoothed onto the flat surface before them.

"Now," Sal said, his voice firm and professional, "we just need to figure out where to stop along the way for refueling."

9

THE PRISON TOWER

The night stretched on and on.

Libby huddled against the door, unable to sleep, unable to even think clearly. She was inside a castle tower, that much she was sure. She had been brought here hours before by the same strange men who had taken her parents to the hospital. They had carried her from the trunk of the car and into a gated courtyard that was completely surrounded by sandstone walls.

She remembered the walls especially: they loomed everywhere, contorting into various towers or bending into arched doorways that led to rooms and hallways, never showing another gap to the world outside. The men had taken her through one of the doorways and up a spiral stairway, higher and higher, before depositing her here, inside a dark, damp room.

All night, she had remained frozen to the spot, too terrified to move, wrapped up in her coat, until signs of morning began to diffuse the night.

Libby stared with a sense of relief at the cracks of sunshine now peeping into the room. The light streamed through a single area where a stack of boards leaned against the wall, and the rays of light were brightly colored, as if filtering through a prism, flecking beams of blue and green and magenta over the bare floor, lighting the room enough to see.

She could tell now that the room was perfectly round, without any sign of electricity. A cot stood in the middle of the floor and a blanket was folded on the ground beside it, and to the back of the room, a small toilet and pedestal sink faced her, without any pretence of privacy. They were the only fixtures to be seen. Above her, exposed rafters soared to at least twenty feet in the air before meeting the conical roof.

Libby hobbled to her feet and tried the door handle, already knowing that it would be locked. It was. She didn't bother to complain, but turned around instead, once more facing her cell. The beams of light continued to dance across the floor, making colorful patterns that changed like a kaleidoscope.

She walked toward the boards and began lifting them away from the wall, stacking them one by one on the ground until the last board had been removed, revealing a round, stained-glass window. The light gushed through it, now brightening the room so that it glowed with color. Eagerly, Libby pushed the boards directly under the window and used them as a step so that she could reach the small latch to its right side. She wiggled the latch until it loosened and carefully pushed the window so that it swung out on its hinge. The blast of icy air overwhelmed her at first, but when her eyes focused, she peered hopefully through the opening. And then she groaned out loud.

While she knew that she was in a tower, she had not realized just how far *above* everything else she was. It was impossible to escape; the changing roof line of the castle lay fifteen or more feet below her, and beyond that, the rolling hills and farmland surrounded by forest spread out to the horizon. No sound or sight of civilization could be seen, except the fact that a narrow ribbon of a road traced its way from the faraway woods to the imposing castle walls.

Libby stared in dismay at the countryside, the frosty air stinging her eyes. She shivered and was just about to close the window when she noticed a motion in the distance, a dark shape moving up the road.

She blinked to focus and now recognized a human form. As the form grew closer, she saw that it was a boy; a boy with dark hair and dark clothing, who was making his way to the castle. She waited impatiently for him to draw nearer, desperate to grab his attention. She could just make out his appearance now: he was pale and appeared to be about her age, maybe a year or so older. He looked tired and hungry, as if he hadn't slept or eaten in days ....

"Help! Help me!" Libby shouted out of the window. A strong wind whipped off the castle walls and drowned out her voice. "Hey, down there! Help me!"

The boy was now nearly at the castle gate. He paused on the bridge and looked around, glancing toward the tower, his big, blue eyes staring up at her in confusion.

"Yes, here!" Libby cried at the top of her lungs. "Help me! I've been kidnapped! Please, you've got to—"

"SSHHHCREEEEAAWW!"

Libby tumbled backwards, falling off the stack of boards and landing on her back as an enormous raven shot through the window. It whooshed over her, slashing its beak through the air as it looped in circles, now stretching its talons toward her face. Instinctively, Libby rolled away and scrambled toward the blanket on the floor, but before she could grab it, the raven swooped once again upon her, now nipping at her arms and legs.

"Go away! Leave me alone!" she screamed, kicking wildly until her foot made contact with something. A groan came from the raven's mouth, which was a very unexpected sound, but Libby was too startled by the raven's attack to really notice it. She did notice, however, that the raven was now lifting away—or rather, floating backwards through the room—its gaze never leaving her face, even as it landed just beside the doorway.

The raven continued to watch her, still and silent, and Libby continued to stare back, panting, unable to look away, and then she forgot all about the boy and the open window because it suddenly seemed to her that the raven was actually ... *changing*.

CHAPTER 9

A peculiar, almost crackling sound filled the room. And then, the raven's feathers began melting, or something similar, more like disappearing really, with white skin showing in its place, and the tips of its wings were changing into thin, long fingers, and its talons were now turning into feet, its head morphing into a human face, and then ....

A man crouched where the raven had been seconds ago. He rubbed a red spot on his throat.

"You have got quite a kick!" he grumbled.

Libby stumbled backwards, recognizing him immediately as one of the men who had carried her to the room last night. The scrawny man continued to rub his throat, his black, beady eyes never leaving her, almost as if he feared she would kick him again, which was ridiculous, of course, because Libby was so gobsmacked by what she had just seen that he could have knocked her over with one of his disappearing feathers.

"Must be those enormous feet," he muttered.

"Who—what—what just happened?" she stammered.

"What a question!" he retorted, throwing her an annoyed glance. "You just bludgeoned the daylights out of me, that is what just happened! Quite unnecessary—I was only trying to get you away from the window!"

Libby blinked.

"Who *are* you?"

"Have I not told you?"

Libby remembered to shake her head.

"Well, my *name*, if that is what you mean, is Iorgu," he glared, fishing into his pocket and pulling out a key.

"I-I don't understand …."

"Only because your mind will not accept the truth."

"But it's impossible."

"What do you know of possibility?"

Libby stared harder at the man and then blinked again.

"And … and you work for *her?*" she finally managed at length. "You work for that horrible woman?"

"Her name is Zelna, and I owe my life to her," corrected Iorgu, picking a sliver from the door with his thin, pale fingers.

Libby gulped, disbelieving that anything, not even a bird who turns into a person, could owe their life to someone so awful, but the man only smiled nostalgically in response, his face relaxing so that he didn't look annoyed any longer.

"She took my brother and me in when we were babies— just two more freaks from a faraway village that no one wanted to be near. I suppose it is a real nuisance when a child switches into a bird every now and again," he smirked before his expression grew pensive. "But my master said that is what she liked about us. She gave us a home and a life," he looked around the tower before resting his dark, empty eyes upon her. "So I strongly suggest you behave yourself and not do anything to upset her. No more attempts to attract attention from strangers or any other silly notions of escape, alright? I will do whatever she commands … no matter what."

Libby nodded to herself and sank onto the ground, her knees shaking the whole way. She couldn't quite comprehend what the man was saying; it was too impossible, and yet, there he was, and here she sat, and just a few moments ago, he had literally flown in through the window.

"Why?" she asked foggily. "I mean, why am I here? Why all this trouble, just to guard me?"

He considered her for a moment, his eyes alert with interest, and then he pivoted towards the door without answering.

"But what about my parents?" called Libby, scrambling to her feet. "What have you done with them? Please, just tell me that!"

Iorgu paused.

"What an interesting subject you are, Liberty Frye," he replied in a murmur. "Here you are, far from home, helpless and locked up in a tower guarded by the likes of *me*, and you're more worried about your parents?"

"Please, just tell me what's happened to them!"

"Well, it is refreshing, but I really do need to attend to my other duties," he tutted. "As you know, we have another visitor downstairs, and it is rude, after all, to keep guests waiting. My brother is perfectly useless in these matters."

"That boy, you mean," said Libby, remembering. "Who is he?"

"Who knows," sighed Iorgu with a shrug. "But he is young and strong and healthy. That is all that usually matters around here."

And for no apparent reason—other than the fact that her parents were presumably dead and she was held captive in a castle tower guarded by a man who, minutes before, had been an entirely different species—Libby's stomach suddenly felt very queasy.

Iorgu smiled, as if he could guess the effect of his presence, and then he turned the door knob.

"I've got to go now," he called. "Please remember what I said about behaving ... it will make things so much easier for both of us."

And with that, he slipped through the doorway, locking it behind him.

Libby remained rooted to the floor, staring after him as his words sank into her mind. For the first time since everything awful had happened, Libby realized that she was completely alone. And much, much more terrifying than that, she knew with that kind of certainty that sinks into one's bones, that she would never see her parents or Uncle Frank or Ginny—or even Buttercup—ever again.

10

ᚢHE ᚢNUSUAL ᚪRRIVAL

Ginny sat, stiff and sore, inside Sal's P-40, the days and nights of travel blurring into each other. She recalled stops in Quebec and Baffin Island, Greenland, Iceland, the Faroe Islands ... she had no idea what day it even was. No matter, for Sal flew his underage cargo onward, into north Scotland, then to Ipswich, England, and now, finally, continental Europe.

Ginny marveled at Sal's incredible connections; he knew at least one person in, what seemed like, every corner of the world. She had to admit that she was surprised he had so many people that, well, *liked* him.

Her thoughts swam tangentially as she recalled the strange night spent inside a sheep farmer's barn on the south coast of

Greenland. A wry smile crossed her face—if Libby could only see this! She wouldn't believe it. *In fact*, thought Ginny, *I'm having a hard time believing it.*

The plane suddenly jolted and she lost her balance, falling over sideways. She struggled to push herself back up and clutched her bag, careful not to let its contents scatter on the floor. It contained the only possessions she had: some clothes, her walkie-talkie, all the money that Uncle Frank had on him (which wasn't a whole lot, considering) and the address of Libby's grandparents. As for the necklace, she had that on her. Uncle Frank had made her promise that she would never take it off.

"It is what will lead you to Libby," he had said.

Sal shouted something back at her, but she couldn't understand him. The roar of the plane throbbed in her ears as she scooted forward to see through the cockpit window ahead of her. They were flying low; Sal appeared to be looking for something.

Ginny hiccupped and swallowed again, suppressing an urge to throw up. She suddenly felt very dizzy … the plane dipped and her stomach popped up into her throat. She closed her eyes tight, trying not to moan. She forced herself to think of other things, of the landing, of her plans, anything but her motion sickness.

"Almost there!" Sal shouted. "Welcome to the State of Hessen, Germany, kid. What you see down there is Frankfurt!"

Bleary eyed, Ginny peered into the cockpit. Sal sat rigid with concentration, his time-weathered hands maneuvering the controls with surprising grace. Ginny squeezed her eyes closed as they swung over sky-scrappers, Sal howling in delight as his plane barreled through the metropolis.

"Will you look at that?" he exclaimed, his voice undeniably awestruck. "This town is completely different! They've rebuilt it all—it's like New York City!"

Ginny rubbed her eyes and peered through the glass canopy. The blue sky floated overhead as the top of what appeared to be another building flashed by. Minutes passed, and then the towering clusters of corporations and banks were replaced with smaller buildings. "Are-are we supposed to be flying so low?" she asked, straining her voice to be heard over the humming plane.

"Of course not!" cackled Sal. "That's what makes it so— OH, CRUD!"

Ginny glanced through the windows and noticed two dark, sleek jets headed directly toward them. "What's going on?" she yelled nervously.

"Looks like they've decided to send us a welcoming party," shouted Sal. "Maybe they don't like me flying so low, either!"

Ginny clasped her hands over her eyes as one of the jets shrieked over them.

"Or maybe, they just don't like my plane," Sal continued to speculate as his plane hurled through the sky, now heading over homes and small, fenced yards.

"What are we going to do?"

"Hang on, kid. Those jets don't look too friendly and we've gotta find a place to land this bird. I'm not sure exactly where we are—I know we're about over Hanau, but everything looks so different!"

"What do you *mean* you don't know where we are?" wailed Ginny.

"Hey, this was your bright idea, remember? Just help me look for a river. The Kinzig should be down there somewhere, and it flows right into Hanau."

The plane swooped over houses and streets as Sal concentrated on the land below him, ignoring the jets escorting him from above.

"River?" Ginny yelled nervously. "We passed a big river a while ago. I don't see how you could've missed it."

"Not that river—that's the Main," shouted Sal over the noise. "We're looking for the Kinzig—much smaller—it flows into the big one at Hanau."

"Oh," said Ginny, feeling overwhelmed and wholly out of her element. She peered frantically through the glass, looking down at the brown, frozen earth neatly squared off with fences and bisected by roads.

"There! There's the river!" she shouted, pointing to the left of the cockpit's window, and just then, the jets shrieked overhead.

"Good job, kid," called Sal, leering through the glass at the prowling jets, and it seemed to Ginny that he might actually be enjoying himself. "It's gonna be a drop and go. Can't get off with you, and you can't wait around, either. Once you land, run like heck into the woods and don't let anyone stop you. And don't forget to radio me once you're safe; we'll figure out where to meet from there."

"You're not coming?" gasped Ginny in disbelief. "You're just going to *drop me off?*"

"What else can I do, kid?" yelled Sal over the noise. "Those jets mean business; I guess they don't like me showing up, all unannounced like. I've got to lose them first, but don't worry, I've got my necklace and the radio, so we're bound to find each other …." His voice disappeared into the roars of the engine as the plane nose-dived toward the earth.

Ginny looked out to see rolling hills approaching at a distressing rate, the descent spinning her mind and turning her stomach. Her head knocked against the back of Sal's seat and she sank down, bracing herself for a crash. The plane continued to wheeze with high-pitched strains before suddenly straightening and then, within seconds, the plane touched the earth, the wheels thumping against the ground and bouncing Ginny from the seat. Her shoulder hit the sidewall as she reached out for something to hold on to, the violent bumping continuing as she steadied herself, pulling with all her might to lift up enough to see out of the canopy.

The plane whooshed through the field as Ginny peered, white faced, through the glass. The frozen ground of winter spread out before them, and gentle hills reached up from the field's boundaries, brown and clustered with trees. A few specks in the sky grew larger, and Ginny's eyes focused to see the jets approaching them from the distance.

"This is it?" she shouted over the engine roar, her voice shaking with her knees. The plane slowed down and turned around in a circle. She glanced through the glass and saw the jets swooping toward them, then circling back up into the air. "I-I'm just supposed to *jump out?*"

"Yep," said Sal, struggling with his seatbelt clip. "You'd better get moving. They'll be coming for me any minute—now, why won't you cooperate?" he snarled at his seatbelt. "A man can fly across the ocean but can't get out of his—there!" The clip finally released and Sal scrambled out of his seat. He reached up and slid back the glass canopy and then turned to Ginny, ready to push her through. She gaped back at him, the chill wind hitting her face like a slap. And then, she started to sob.

"Now's the wrong time to start with *that*, kid! You've gotta go!"

"But-but, wh-what am I *doing* here?" she gasped, tears of panic streaming down her face. "I've changed my mind! I want to go back!"

"Snap out of it!" bellowed Sal, and the sound of his voice must have helped because Ginny stopped blubbering long enough to listen. "You're on a darn mission, kid, that's what you're doing here, and you don't have much time! The cops will be here soon, and as you can see, I've already got a situation. That's better. Now, remember what we talked about—go straight for the woods. Harder time finding you there. Wait a couple of hours until it clears before coming out again. Radio me and follow the river toward Hanau. I'll figure out a way to meet up with you there. Don't worry."

Ginny felt herself nodding as she buttoned her coat with trembling fingers. She blinked rapidly, suddenly aware that her tears were actually freezing around her eyes. And then she felt the straps of her bag being slipped over her shoulders, the movement causing the stone necklace to thump lightly upon her chest.

She took a deep breath and, with a shaky step, climbed through the open canopy, out onto the plane wing, not quite believing that she really was here and that she really was about to run into the middle of the woods, all alone, smack dab in the center of Germany.

"Gotta go!" he shouted after her. "I'll find you as soon as I can!"

She crouched at the edge of the wing to jump, but then she slipped and fell belly-first to the ground.

"Good luck, kid," Sal called from the cockpit, his voice barely audible above the noise. "Now, RUN!"

Ginny blinked, lifting up her head to see the two jet planes swooping down again. She crawled to her feet, shaking so much that all she could do was concentrate on not collapsing, and then she turned toward the woods. Behind her, she heard the sound of Sal's plane revving up.

"Run, run, run, run!" she wailed to herself, feeling tears streaking down her cheeks once again. The sound of sirens blared somewhere behind her.

She ran on, now inside the woods, her lungs burning from the cold air and her legs rubbery from the flight. She forced herself to press on, wheezing and gasping as she went, wobbling between trees and slipping on the frozen ground. She thought she heard the sound of shouting far behind her.

"Matter of life and death—must keep running," she sobbed, wiping her eyes with her sleeve. She was now running up a hill, her heart and lungs burning almost beyond endurance as the sound of shouting grew louder. She reached the hill's crest and saw that the river was some seven feet below, cutting off her route. Its swift, icy current boiled over jagged rocks before disappearing over a ledge about fifty feet away.

The sound of barking and more shouting grew closer and Ginny turned to see a man in a greyish-green uniform bounding through the trees toward her, followed by two German shepherds. Ginny gasped and looked from them to the frothing river and back again. The officer grew closer and the dogs passed him, now galloping up the hill, flecks of white spit flicking from their mouths, teeth bared.

Ginny looked back at the river and scuttled along the crest, searching for a place to climb down. The water roared in her ears as she turned once more to see the man closing in on her—he was calling to the dogs and they slowed down, their teeth disappearing in disappointment, but the man kept running, his eyes locked on Ginny. She crouched, frozen, as if under a spell, watching in slow motion as the man in the green uniform ran up to her. She could hear his ragged breath, the sounds of the dogs' excited barking ringing oddly in her ears; she could see the man reaching out his hand to her, his expression full of astonishment ....

A terrific roar filled the sky and both Ginny and the man looked up to see a gaping mouth with sharp, white teeth swooping over them, the face of a hungry shark descending from the sky. The man shouted excitedly and Ginny shouted too, only she was wailing for the plane to come back and get her, but then, just as quickly, Sal's P-40 swooped upwards once more, tearing away through the clouds.

The policeman muttered and shook his head, forcing his attention back to the blubbering, freckle-faced fugitive who, he just noticed, was having some trouble on the icy slope.

"*Whooaaaooo!*" cried Ginny, her feet slipping from under her, and then she tumbled over the bluff before the policeman could even respond.

Down she went, screaming the whole way, until the rushing, icy needles of the river knocked the breath from her. She looked up, shocked by the water that was so cold that it felt as though it were setting her legs and arms on fire … the tangle of leafless bushes passed swiftly by, the blur of muted, frozen colors … so cold, the burning … the man on the hill growing more and more distant … she could hardly breathe … and then, nothing.

The man in the greyish-green uniform stood on the hill's crest. A horrified expression shadowed his face as he caught sight of a brown head bobbing briefly upon the river's surface before disappearing over the steep, furious edge.

11

THE BLACK CAULDRON

Over a week had come and gone. Libby remained locked in her tower, pacing the floor of her cell during the day and peering out of the window, hoping for another sign of life from the world outside.

None came.

And what about that boy she had seen? Libby asked herself for the hundredth time. She had watched him approach the gate all those days ago, but then, she never saw him *leave*. In fact, she hadn't seen anyone since then, not even Iorgu. Even her food was brought to her during the few hours at night that she slept. If it hadn't been for that, she'd assume she'd been completely forgotten.

A nervous, high-pitched giggle interrupted her thoughts, its sound drawing nearer as it floated up the tower stairs. Libby's pulse quickened. She'd been waiting for another chance, and this time, she'd be prepared.

Libby darted toward the window and grabbed one of the boards stacked on the floor. It was too wide for her to get a decent grip, but she didn't have a choice in the matter now because the jangle of keys rang from the other side of her cell.

The door swung open.

A man peered into the room, his eyes twitching nervously as he looked around for Libby. Was it Iorgu or the other one? Libby didn't wait to find out.

"Take *that*!" she shouted, swinging with all of her might at the intruder, but the board was too heavy, and it went flying out of her hands before she could regain control of it. What happened next seemed like it was all in slow motion: The man screamed and threw his hands in the air, flinging away the tray of food he held in the process. The board hurtled across the room, smashing into the falling tray, and in the next instant, a not-so-baked potato (because, as a general rule, prisoners don't get properly cooked food) was barreling toward the screaming man. Something crunched and the man fell to his knees.

"Oh, my nose!" he shrieked, bringing his hands to his face.

For a split second, Libby gaped in disbelief at the howling man, stunned by the devastation that a simple, unassuming potato could cause, and then she remembered that she was trying to escape.

She darted through the open doorway, slammed the door

closed, twisted the key in the lock and dashed down the winding stairwell, circling lower and lower until she reached the empty courtyard. She sprinted toward the gate where she remembered being carried through days before, and her heart was racing, she didn't know what she was doing, but it didn't matter because when she reached the gate, she saw that it was locked, and that the sides of it were actually built into the castle's outer wall, making it impossible to climb over or squeeze through.

She ran back to the center of the courtyard, looking around for another way out. She was completely surrounded by the labyrinth of walls, towers and doors, with no indication of an alternative exit … the smell of freshly baked bread caught her attention. It had been a whole day since she'd last eaten, and the aroma made her stomach growl loudly.

"Kitchens often lead to the outside," she realized, thinking of their garden back home, and for a moment her heart ached from the memory of it, of her mother, who was always there, always planting funny herbs she'd never heard of ….

"Not now," she whispered, gritting her teeth, and she followed the scent through one of the arched doorways, suddenly finding herself within a long, narrow hall that curved along the inside of the castle wall. Behind her, several open doorways could be seen leading from the hallway into other rooms, but Libby continued forward, following the smell of bread until she reached an enormous, wooden door. It was cracked open ever so slightly, and the glow of an open fire could be seen crackling from a stone fireplace; a thick, wooden table stood in the middle of the room, loaded with potatoes, a block of cheese and a basket full of bread rolls. A radio on the table jingled out holiday songs. Her stomach grumbled again.

A movement from inside made her shrink from the door. She sank into the darkness just in time to watch a fat cook waddle into the hallway with a large tray; Libby remained pressed into the shadows, watching after the cook until she disappeared around the corner.

The smell of bread hit her again and this time, it was more than she could bear. She edged toward the kitchen and darted inside.

Firelight flickered off the yellow-rust colored walls and she could now see that, to the right of the fireplace, the kitchen continued on another fifteen or so feet. One side of the room was covered from the height of her waist to several feet above her head with various utensils: spoons, knives, cutting boards, ladles, forks ....

Libby grabbed two rolls, stuffing one into her mouth and chewing as fast as she could while examining the walls, hoping to find some sort of window or doorway leading outside.

Besides the normal kitchen instruments and an unusual assortment of knives, several other items hung on the wall as well, one being a gigantic tong with a rounded globe end, and another looked like a huge pair of tweezers—nearly two feet long—that hung with a certain menacing air from a large, black hook.

She grimaced and continued around the room, glancing

into the shadows for any sign of an exit, when she nearly toppled over a large, iron kettle sitting on the floor. A wave of something odd hit her nostrils. She held her nose and peered into the cauldron, straining to see through the increasing darkness of the room. Something was definitely in there ... something bobbing on the surface. She leaned in further. The roll fell from her hands, plopping into the water. And then Libby realized what was floating beside her soggy bread roll:

It was the head of a boy, *the* boy, the one she had seen from her window, with bulging blue eyes and dark brown hair, staring straight up at her. Libby stared back at it, unable to look away, unable to even move, until she became aware of the sound of her voice. She clapped her hands over her mouth, trying to stifle her screams, but it was too late. Something moved above her. She looked up.

"Zelna," she gulped.

And then, she was being dragged through the kitchen, Zelna had her around the middle, carrying her as if she were nothing more than a basket of dirty laundry, moving through the hallway, now across the courtyard and up the winding stairwell, her feet clunking on the steps until she landed with a thud on the floor of her cell.

Zelna loomed above her in the darkness, her long, dark skirts towering into the space above as the regal head with glowing emerald eyes slowly came into view, and even in her state of shock, Libby realized that, once again, she looked different. Only this time, it was for the opposite reason: Zelna's eyes seemed brighter somehow, and as she drew closer, Libby could see that her hair was darker—jet black, without any hint of grey—and the way she moved was as of that of an athlete, tall and strong, with none of the signs of age that she had shown at her grandmother's house ....

The image of the cauldron flashed into her mind once more, instantly burning away any other thought. She suddenly felt that she was going to throw up.

"He came to me, you know. It vas not as if I sought him out," drifted Zelna's voice, and before Libby could collect herself to speak, Zelna nodded her head in understanding, and murmured, *"You already know vhy."*

Libby only moaned in response, rocking back and forth, too distraught to wonder how this horrible woman could reply to things she hadn't asked out loud. Zelna bent lower, so that her face was now only inches away, and she grabbed Libby by her jaw, forcing her gaze up.

"Just look at me!" she said, and there was pride in the command. "Do I look aged, helpless like your grandmother? Do I look eighty? Seventy ... even sixty?"

"No," whispered Libby. "You look—"

"Young!" finished Zelna, releasing her grasp. "But even this magic is fleeting. And it comes at a price ... to others."

"And, and you really do—" stammered Libby, still not quite able to accept the ghastly truth behind her words, but there was no other way to explain what she had seen in that cauldron. "You *eat* children, just like in the fairy tales? That's what you do?"

"We all must survive somehow," answered Zelna. "Even vitches have certain needs."

"Witches?" repeated Libby in disbelief, because *that* was impossible. So much had happened in such little time, but the one thing she was sure of, was that witches didn't exist. *And neither do birds that turn into humans*, she reminded herself, but Zelna was rolling her eyes in response, as if it were ridiculous to acknowledge something so obvious. Libby swallowed hard; it felt like a balloon had inflated in her throat. "So, is that what you plan to do to me?" she managed to ask.

Zelna considered her for a long moment, her eyes filling with an eagerness that made Libby's pulse freeze. And then she said:

"You and I are not so different, Liberty Frye."

Libby peered up at the woman, for the moment too shocked to remember her terror. And the memory of her parents gushed back into her mind with a force that swelled inside her, like a wind filling an enormous sail.

"Not so *different!*" she repeated, wobbling to her feet. The air from the open window wafted across her face and the briskness helped clear her head somewhat.

Memories of that last day with her parents came flooding back, of the way they were carted off, of the way she was tricked into staying at the house. Maybe if she had gone with them, maybe she could have saved them somehow. Maybe they would still be alive and wouldn't be kept away from her, in some wretched place, without any way of knowing what had really happened ....

A sob rolled out of her and she was suddenly seized with such fury that she didn't care anymore, she wasn't even afraid anymore.

"You and I are about as *different* as *different* can get!" Libby spat, and her hands curled into fists that shook at her sides; she wanted nothing more than to charge at Zelna and punch her, smash her with anything she could. "You've killed my parents and-and you eat children and … who knows *what* else, and you look at me and you tell me we aren't so *different?"* she raged, and tears welled up in her eyes, and she hated her, hated her, hated her. "You are worse than evil, worse than anything I can imagine, and you won't get away with this!" she choked furiously. "I don't know how, but I know you won't!"

But to her astonishment, Zelna only laughed with delight, the sound like glass shattering against tiled floors—cold and clean and unfeeling.

"That is more like it!" she exclaimed. "That is the spirit I want—it vill give me something to vork for!"

Libby could only glare back, utterly confounded by the horrible person before her.

"You are a defiant one," Zelna continued to observe, her voice neither approving nor disapproving.

"Why am I here?" Libby choked out.

"Vhy indeed?" smiled the woman.

"But then," Libby swallowed hard, attempting to control the sudden thumping in her chest, because there was something very disconcerting about the way Zelna looked at her, "what exactly is it that you have planned for me?"

"You vill simply have to vait and see," she answered coolly. "You have your grandmother to thank for it, by the vay. Had she not botched things up years ago, you vouldn't be in this situation," and then Zelna ran her fingers down a slender chain that looped at her waist, pulling up a timepiece. She gazed down at it, frowning, now moving towards the door. Libby stared after her, too overwhelmed and confused to fully account for the random ideas that popped into her head.

"Orange flavored."

Zelna stopped at the doorway and raised her left eyebrow ever so slightly. "Pardon?"

Libby cleared her throat.

"I was just thinking that you … eat children as if they were simply vitamins," she answered hoarsely. "Like those orange flavored ones."

"Not a bad comparison," Zelna shrugged, reaching for the handle. "But even I grow tired of vitamins."

"And my parents," Libby called, forcing herself to focus, "if they aren't … vitamins … to you, then why did you take them?"

"Your parents are not vhat I vould be concerned vith," she replied, glancing again at her watch. "Now, it is late and you need to get your rest. After all, it vould not do either of us much good for you to get sick."

She reached into her pocket, pulling out a small object that slipped from her fingers and rolled across the room toward Libby. A wispy vapor eked over the floor.

CHAPTER 11

"Sleep tight, little niece."

"Wait …." Libby struggled to think of something, anything. But her mind grew fuzzy and her eyelids felt heavy, so heavy, and what was it that she had just said ….

12

MIDNIGHT FLIGHT

The tunnel was pitch-black, with only the glow of a curious, floating orb to navigate through the darkness. It appeared to her while she slept, and she followed it without saying a word, almost without even waking, and to her astonishment, she found she could step right through the walls of her cell, as if they were merely phantoms.

She continued following the orb until she found herself within a tunnel; she didn't know where she was going, but she knew she was climbing downward, and she knew that the orb was leading somewhere she must go to save her parents and, for some reason, Ginny too, and even Buttercup. She knew they were all locked away someplace deep and dark and that it was up to her to find them ....

"Liberty Frye," a voice whispered, and Libby squinted into the darkness, suddenly realizing that her orb had disappeared. The darkness closed about her, and it felt as though it were sucking something from the air she breathed. It circled closer and closer; she tried to move, but her arms and legs felt pinned to her sides and the darkness drew nearer and she knew that any moment now, it would be too late ....

"Liberty Frye," the voice whispered again, and it touched something in her mind, like a finger reaching into her thoughts. "I'm sorry to do this, but I was afraid you would fight me," the voice continued; it sounded nervous. "Do not worry, I am strong enough."

A blast of air hit her face, forcing her eyes wide open. Libby gasped again, only this time, the air was sharp and jarring and it instantly cleared her head. She realized she'd been sleeping—that the orb and the tunnel had all been a dream. And then, she opened her mouth to scream, because she discovered that she was actually flying through the cold night sky—gliding really—and she heard a rhythmic strumming above her, like the beating of wings, and below her, there was ... absolutely nothing.

No, it was impossible. She must still be asleep, she told herself, but she could feel the frosty air stinging her cheeks and she could see that, inexplicably, she had on her red, wool coat. It was buttoned all the way up so that it pulled against her throat, and she could wiggle her hands and her feet, although it was true that they were constricted somehow, but no, no, no, it was still all a dream ....

The air streamed past her and she became aware that she was surrounded by stars, and that, somewhere in the dark void below her, slept the unlit countryside. She felt the grip of something on her back; it was strong and it held her like a piece of dangling fruit, carrying her through the darkness, now lower and lower, down, down, down, until the shadowy hint of forest was seen.

She tried to call out, no longer afraid of the flying but rather, of the rapid descent and of the trees rushing past her, but she realized that her mouth was gagged and that her arms were tied somehow so that she could not raise them. She watched helplessly as the ground came into view, but then to her surprise, right before she should have collided face-first into the frozen earth, the descent stopped so that she floated once more in space. And then, she was gently lowered to the ground.

Libby lay astonished on the forest floor, too amazed to think straight for a full minute. From behind her, she heard shuffling followed by a crackling sound. Moments later, a pale face appeared.

"You!" she exclaimed, but her words were muffled from the gag in her mouth. The man now circled around her, busily untying the rope about her arms and legs.

"I am sorry for giving you such a shock," he whispered anxiously, "but I did not know another way to do this. I knew you would not trust me, and there is no time to lose," he glanced up at the sky, his face twitching eerily. "It is nearly dawn, and you will only have a few hours of daylight," he continued, his tone urgent. "You are in the woods of Rodenbach now, Liberty Frye. You must follow the path here until you find what looks like the ruins of an abbey. You cannot miss it. There, you will find a woman named Sabine."

Libby struggled to a sitting position and stared hard at the man before her.

"She is a witch also, but she deals in a different craft," he explained calmly, as if depositing a girl in the middle of a German forest with instructions to encounter a witch was a perfectly normal thing to do. "She is the only one who can help you now."

Libby gulped and tried to speak, but the gag remained in her mouth and the rope remained bound about her wrists. Her head ached horribly.

"I will untie you now, but you must promise not to scream," said the man. "For your own sake, please, you must be quiet."

Libby nodded, and the man eyed her once more, as if unsure as to whether or not he believed her, but he loosened the gag all the same.

"Which one are you?" she gasped as soon as she could. "Iorgu?"

The man shook his head, now tugging at the knots about her wrists.

"I am Emil," he murmured. "We … met yesterday."

Libby rubbed her wrists where the rope had been. Then she pinched herself. It hurt. She was definitely awake. And if that wasn't proof enough, the man before her sported a large, purple welt over the bridge of his nose, exactly where he might have been cudgeled by one rogue, under-baked potato.

"Why should I trust you?" she said through the fogginess of her mind. "How do I know you're not trying to trick me?"

"But you do not have any other choice."

Libby bit her lip and thought about this for a moment.

"Well, why now?" she wavered, gesturing about her. "Why now, like this, in the middle of the night?"

"Because even I have my limits, and I have long fought my conscience over what I have been a part of, all in the name of loyalty," he responded, and there was an earnestness to his voice that made her listen. "Besides, I tried to tell you of my plan yesterday, but you broke my nose before I had a chance to."

"I'm sorry; I was trying to escape—"

"No time for apologies," said Emil. "Listen, you must find Sabine, and you must tell her that your parents are hidden in the Devil's Cave, under the spell of deep sleep. She will know what to do. She knew your mother once, a long time ago."

"Deep sleep," repeated Libby, struggling to compose her frazzled thoughts, and then her mind instantly sharpened. "*Deep sleep?*" she repeated again, only this time with dramatically increased enthusiasm. "As in ... not dead?" she cried, scrambling to her feet. "They're still alive?"

"Of course they're not dead," he responded in surprise.

"They're really *alive?*"

"Well, I don't know how else to put it ...."

"You're *sure?*"

"Yes, but, please, you have only a few hours left before it is too late, Liberty Frye," he replied politely, clearly baffled by her reaction. "You must focus. There are still many things to be done!" and then he yelped in alarm because Libby was hugging him and jumping up and down at the same time and something warm and wet was trickling down his cheek.

"Thank you, thank you," she gasped, hugging him even tighter, and somewhere in the huddle, Emil's muffled protests could be heard.

"You ... leaking."

Libby didn't notice, because she was soaring, soaring, soaring and her heart was somewhere above her head, somewhere beyond the stars, even. She wouldn't have noticed if a humongous, ancient tree had quite inexplicably moved several inches from its original spot and now leaned its branches to the ground, as if bowing before her, which, in fact, one just had ....

"Please," Emil gasped, frantically trying to disengage himself. He struggled to his feet and pushed her away. "Please stop all of this emotion! No, no, you must follow my directions and go!"

Libby hiccupped and then blinked rapidly.

"You—you're not coming?"

"I must leave now," he replied. "I have been gone too long as it is. It is already morning and there is no time to lose, my friend. Now, hurry!"

Libby sniffled and wiped her face.

"But what about you?"

Emil merely looked warily back at her, and Libby glanced down at the ground, suddenly feeling ridiculous. Clearly, her outburst had unnerved him.

"Well, thank you," she said, holding out her hand in a businesslike manner, but Emil just stared at it, as if he'd never seen such a custom as a handshake. Libby tucked her hand back into her coat pocket and cleared her throat. "I don't understand half of what is going on, or why you're even doing this …." She stopped, feeling her emotions well up inside her again, and she fought to keep them under control. "But from the bottom of my heart, thank you," she managed to finish.

"Thank me by saving yourself," said Emil, turning abruptly away. "You have much to prove before this is all over, but I believe you are capable. You have a strength about you that gives you courage."

"I don't *feel* courageous at all," admitted Libby.

"That does not matter as much; it matters more what you do about it. I have learned that the hard way. But you must trust in yourself, and only in that, until you and your family are safe from danger," Emil warned. "Even Sabine should be regarded with some level of suspicion. Even I …." His voice trailed off, and he shook his head once more. "Well, I know what I *hope* I will do, but who knows? You must go now while you still have a chance."

Dazedly, Libby watched after him as he stepped into the shadows behind the trees, a thousand questions racing through her mind. From where she stood, she heard the strange, shuffling sound followed by odd, muted crackling.

CHAPTER 12

"Good bye, Liberty Frye."

And then, seconds later, she saw the form of a raven rising into the air, barely perceptible against the velvet darkness.

13

The Witch in the Woods

L ibby continued down the forest path, oblivious to the strange noises and movements about her: the shifting trees, the oddly whispering breeze that actually sounded more like words than of rustling foliage. She was too focused on Emil's words, repeating them over to herself so that she would not forget.

She soon approached a small meadow that glowed uncannily under the waning moonlight. Her pulse quickened at the sight of an ancient, stone tower rising from the center of it, and just beyond that, slightly to the side, was a low-lying hut made of the same stone. A chimney could be seen from this last structure, and the smell of smoke filled the air. A circle of stonework surrounded it all, comprised of huge boulders placed back to back, each fitting into a peculiar groove with the other.

"The abbey ruins," Libby whispered, hugging her coat tighter against her body. Her frosty breath nearly crystallized in the air and she was immediately aware of the cold—she could barely even feel her fingers—and just the smell of the fire made her anxious for its warmth. She took another deep breath, exhaling slowly, and then climbed over the boulders, into the clearing.

"Hello?" she called softly.

She walked toward the stone hut and reached out to knock upon the door, but as soon as she made contact, the door swung open, exposing the glow of firelight from inside.

"Hello?" she called again, leaning through the doorway. "I'm sorry for intruding, but I am looking for—"

Libby fell against the wall, too shocked to turn and run.

The fireplace threw light over the opposite side of the room, and Libby saw an old woman, dressed in a shabby robe, with wild, long, white hair and bulbous, grey eyes looming before her. She was horrifically ugly, with rotten teeth and skin that looked as if it may actually be decaying right off her face, and somewhere in the terrified sequence of her thoughts, it occurred to Libby that if she had ever imagined what a real-life witch would look like, it would be this woman.

"Wer sind Sie?" wheezed the woman in astonishment. "Was wünschen Sie?"

"I'm so sorry, ma'am, but I don't speak German, er, Deutsch!" Libby blundered desperately. "I'm looking for Sabine!"

The woman fell silent and gazed about her in confusion.

"I'm the daughter of Peter and Gretchen Frye," Libby continued, hoping for any sign of recognition from the woman. "Gretchen … von Strauss?" she tried again, using her mother's maiden name.

The woman continued to stare blankly for a moment, and then her expression changed, as if a light had flickered somewhere in her thoughts.

"I'm Liberty Frye," Libby persisted, but she was beginning to worry that she was in the wrong place. "I've come for your help! My parents, they—"

"Liberty Frye?" repeated the woman.

"Er, yes," answered Libby in confusion. "I—"

"Well, why didn't you just say so in the first place?"

"But I—"

"Come, come!" the woman exclaimed, shuffling over to close the door, and then she grabbed Libby by the arm and tugged her toward the fireplace, kicking away the piles of books and papers that were scattered about the floor. An old, white dog lay in the middle of the mess, apparently too worn out to do much more than lift a droopy eyelid as Libby staggered past.

"Are you Sabine, then?" Libby asked as she wove between the clutter. She was having trouble keeping her eye on the pathway between the books; there was an astonishing assortment of strange things to look at, not the least of which were collections of preserved frogs that hung in random clusters from the ceiling, like garlands of kitchen garlic.

"Who else?" answered the woman. "What a silly question."

"And—and, you speak English," Libby sighed in relief.

"Of course; most of us do, you know," she gestured at a seat by the hearth that was covered with some sort of dried plant material. Libby looked down at it dubiously.

"Sit!" she commanded, and Libby sank onto the crunchy surface, too bewildered to question anything at this point. "Liberty Frye, it is about time you made it!" continued the woman excitedly. "What took you so long?"

"But I don't—"

"Tardiness is not a trait we witches tolerate," she scolded, "and the stars, well, there's absolutely no justifying yourself to them."

"But that doesn't—"

"Precision is absolutely vital, so you might as well learn how to show up when you're expected! Why, I've lost a whole night of sleep waiting up for you!"

"But you didn't even—"

"But I didn't even what?" snapped Sabine, turning the full force of her hideous gaze on her visitor. Libby gulped, trying hard to politely look away as she struggled to regain her composure.

"For the sake of Kreitenzeilger, speak, child!" cried the woman. "When someone of your stature shows up at my home in the wee hours of the morning, I expect something more than half sentences!"

Libby was so baffled that she nearly burst into tears.

"But you won't let me get a word in edgewise!" she finally blurted.

"Well, that's a start at least."

"Excuse me," Libby paused to collect herself. "What I mean to say is … and this may sound like a dumb question to you … but how do you even know about me?"

Sabine stared back at her in silence, and it was clear that she was seriously beginning to question her visitor's intelligence.

"Do you know who you are?" she finally demanded.

"Of course I know who I am," frowned Libby. "That's what I've been trying to tell you!"

"Well?"

"Well …." Libby scrunched her brows together, desperately trying to understand what exactly Sabine was waiting to hear. "Well, I'm Libby, as you seem to already know, the daughter of Peter and Gretchen Frye … and I—I mean, we—came here for Christmas because my mother wanted to visit my dying grandfather, but things have gone horribly wrong and I've been kidnapped and they're being kept in some sort of cave and are in terrible danger and so I've come to you for help."

Sabine held up a warty finger.

"But you are not *just* the daughter of Peter and Gretchen Frye."

"Okay," sighed Libby, rubbing her neck for a moment, because she just realized it was cramping awfully, "I guess I'm also a ten-year-old girl from Mississippi … who's just escaped from a castle tower, via an *extremely* unnatural method," she added with increasing exasperation, "in order to find a woman who is supposed to help me save my parents!"

CHAPTER 13

"Well that, too," answered Sabine with a dismissive wave of the hand. "But what I'm trying to say is that, well ... you're Liberty Frye!"

Libby slumped against the seat, ignoring the disconcerting crunch against her back.

"Glad we've cleared that up."

"*The* Liberty Frye," persisted Sabine, her voice filling with awe. "I learned of your arrival from the trees! We've been expecting you!"

"You mean, you and ... and the *trees* ... have been expecting me."

"Of course! After all, you are the last of your kind, don't you know? You come from a long line of witch nobility—you've been the subject of conversation for years!"

"Witch ... nobility?"

"All the trees here know about you," nodded Sabine with rather alarming enthusiasm. "You've caused quite a stir; it isn't every day when the descendant of such a distinguished coven returns to her homeland; you've finally completed their chart! They absolutely hate it when family trees are left unfinished, you know. You should just see how they fret and gripe about it," she snickered, exposing a few wobbly teeth. "But now, thanks to you, the genealogy is complete!"

"The genealogy of ... witches," clarified Libby.

"Precisely," beamed the woman. "Lousenfeifer?"

"Oh," Libby glanced distractedly at the bowl Sabine jabbed toward her. "Um, no thank you."

Sabine shrugged and dipped a crooked finger into the bowl,

pulling out a long, bluish object that wriggled a bit like a slug. She popped it into her mouth and began to chew.

"And the trees keep up with this sort of thing," resumed Libby, trying very hard not to gag. "Witch … genealogy and other such related matters?"

"Oh, they keep up with everything," confirmed Sabine, smacking her lips with relish. She dipped into the bowl again. "They're the wisest of all and are experts in every field, if you pardon the pun," she chuckled, and a little trickle of blue ran down the side of her chin. "But don't worry, you're quite safe from Zelna finding out where you are from *them*; they won't speak to her, not after what she did to poor old Barvultmir," she stopped abruptly, as if holding back her words, and a darkness crossed over her face. She bit the corner of her lower lip and looked back at Libby thoughtfully.

"And so, just to clarify what you're telling me," managed Libby, struggling to comprehend the bizarreness of it all, "you *are* saying that—um—that I'm descended from a line of *witches?*"

"Not just any line," corrected the woman, dabbing at her mouth with the edge of her sleeve. "Of the Coven of Hessen, the strongest and most able of us all. Why, you're practically famous! But you would still have to learn, mind you, and more than that, you have to earn it, you know, even someone like you. Just because you have the power in your veins does not mean you get to march out of here and try your *Listineous Heisenduelden* on anything that walks by," cackled Sabine, clearly humored by the notion. "Hoo, hoo, hoo! That would be a sight indeed!"

Libby swallowed.

"Although it does rather surprise me that your mother never told you; I had assumed your birthday would have marked the perfect occasion," Sabine considered. "I taught her, you know," she added with obvious pride. "Secretly, of course."

There was no doubt. Libby was positive the woman before her was completely insane.

"My *mother?*"

"My dear, you do need to keep up!"

"Was a *witch?*"

"Is a witch, my dear. Or, at least, almost one."

"But—but, she's a *baker!*"

"All part of the double cover," agreed Sabine sanguinely.

"Double cover?"

"Of course!" Sabine replied, clearly shocked by Libby's unfamiliarity on the subject. "Someone of our—shall we say, 'status'? I do love code words, don't you? Someone of our status can't go around in the real world reciting runes and reading potion books at the local coffee shop, you know. Not to mention our snacks!" Sabine raised her bowl toward Libby, accidentally slinging part of its contents over the edge. "People would think we're strange! No, no, it simply wouldn't do. The world is not ready for the truth. People would rather believe in a reality that does not exist rather than see what's really there."

Libby stared in dismay at the slimy blue spot on her shoe.

"She was just about to earn her first title when it all happened," Sabine added, and then she took to glaring at a collection of shaved toenails that were neatly sorted by size and color into various glass beakers.

"When what happened?" asked Libby.

Sabine swirled one of the beakers with a long, knobby finger and sighed. "What I'm saying is, that it takes commitment, a lifetime of training and dedication," she finished gloomily. "And even then, well it is different for each of us."

Libby blinked rapidly, a billion questions racing through her mind, but she fought the urge to ask them. She had to focus—she wasn't here to listen to Sabine's outlandish theories, and anyway, it was ridiculous. There was no way her mom could be a witch. Or, fine, a witch in training.

"And so you've learned of me from the trees," Libby resumed, hoping to get Sabine back on track, and the sound of her words rang ridiculously in her ears.

"You're catching on!" nodded Sabine in relief.

"And the trees have told you … what, exactly?"

"That you're in great danger, of course! Goodness, girl, isn't that why you're here, after all? You act as if you don't know anything!"

"That's probably because I don't," replied Libby helplessly. "If you'd just let me—"

"Of course, it hasn't been at all decided, you know," continued Sabine, her eyes shining once again with excitement. "And even the stars can only tell us of what is, not of what is to come, for that changes every second, naturally, as is the nature of all living things. It is part of what makes our work so interesting … and difficult," she sighed.

Libby pressed her fingertips to her eyes for a moment, once again aware of the throbbing in her temples.

"So, what you're saying is that, you've heard of me ... and you've heard that I'm in danger, but you don't know what I'm in danger *of* or what will happen?"

"Well, I know that Zelna and your grandmother certainly have a hand in it," sniffed Sabine. "Why else in the world would your mother have brought you here? I would never have believed it! Never! She must have been bewitched, induced—something she never even saw coming—but it isn't quite clear to me," she muttered, her brows furrowing in frustration.

"Well that makes two of us," said Libby, who was now thoroughly confused, but Sabine continued muttering to herself, and then something she had just said clicked in Libby's mind. "The yellow envelope!" Libby whispered, remembering the strange way her mother had acted that day. "There was a letter ...."

"Of course there was a *letter,*" snapped Sabine, glancing up impatiently. "I'm not completely inept, you know; I just can't see what it *was!* It must have been very clever, oh yes, something insidious—something you wouldn't even notice until it had done its job on the mind—that is Zelna's handiwork right there, oh, but it's no use!" she glowered, wringing her hands in agitation. "I can't see it, girl, and that is that! I don't have the sort of ... skill, for lack of a better word, that your kind take so much for granted!" And then she threw a nasty look Libby's way.

"*I* don't take it for granted," gulped Libby, who really had no idea how she was supposed to respond. "I don't even know what you mean."

But Sabine dismissed her with another wave of her bony hand. "Oh, it's alright, I'm only a rote witch, and I'm fine with that, really I am. I am not like you—I was never born with the power of our craft literally running in my blood; no, I must rely upon other sources to create my magic. But sometimes, sheer force of will can compensate for what nature doesn't give you," she grinned and then immediately looked away, as if aware of how alarming the appearance of a grinning witch must be.

"It has been my life's passion," she resumed somberly, "and so I have learned many things, and I can speak to the trees and I can read the stars, but I cannot see much more beyond what is already there. Few can, and even they, as I already said, can never be certain. It all depends on our choices, you see."

"Sure," said Libby, but it came out as a croak.

"Take Zelna, for instance," continued Sabine. "She is descended of your line, as is your grandmother, of course, who, incidentally, did absolutely nothing with it, but I digress. Zelna and I studied together as children, you see. There was a school here, a secret society for those who wished to learn the ancient ways of Hexenkunst, and it soon became apparent that your great aunt's skill far surpassed any other," Sabine grew silent for a moment, and the glow of the fire danced across the distorted contours of her face.

"So it's true, she really is my *aunt?*" shuddered Libby.

"Of course, dear, didn't you know?"

Libby shook her head slowly.

"She's the elder of the two, you know—ten years Giselle's senior, but they couldn't be more at ends than Viltzila and Rutamute," chuckled Sabine. "Well anyway, Zelna eventually left the school altogether to pursue her own studies; she disappeared for years without a trace, and rumor had it that she was learning the shadow arts, things that even the strongest and most experienced of us refrain from, for the power is so great that it overcomes even those with the purest motive."

"I've seen what she is capable of," whispered Libby, and the events from yesterday came tumbling back in her mind. "I know that she ... she actually *eats children*. This must sound crazy, but somehow, their, um, their youth is transferred into her. I've seen the head of a boy ...." A wave of queasiness rolled up her throat, and she tried to swallow it down.

Sabine nodded calmly as she continued to look into the fire.

"I have heard of these things," she said. "But I've no power to stop her; I doubt anyone can, at least, at present," she paused to glance at Libby, a peculiar expression shifting across her face, and then she immediately straightened her posture, as if forcing her mind away from whatever thought dwelled within. "Which leads me to your plight, you see," she resumed. "Your parents are held at the Devil's Cave—I know the place from my childhood; it is right by the town of Steinau, which just happens to be where Jacob and Wilhelm Grimm grew up."

"The Grimm Brothers?" cut in Libby with surprise, immediately thinking of her book, and she wondered if she should bring the matter up with Sabine....

"Who else?" Sabine said absently, continuing on as if Libby had not interrupted, "and old Tufelwog has already told me how they were poisoned with widgewood, of course."

"Tufelwog?" Libby echoed in bewilderment.

"Oh, he's that magnificent elm," Sabine answered. "You passed under him on your way here."

"Right," said Libby, clearing her throat. "Of course they all have names. And ... widgewood?"

"Why, it's the herb that was slipped to your parents!"

"The Christmas strudel," Libby murmured, but then she immediately closed her mouth because Sabine was leaning toward her, and her breath was absolutely disgusting.

"Your parents remain in a deep sleep," Sabine wheezed, "and tonight ... well, you've really cut it close, Liberty Frye, for tonight marks the Solstice of Aramaar!"

Libby was certain she had never heard of the Solstice of Aramaar, but since she was holding her breath, it made it difficult to politely ask any questions.

"In our craft, it is the most important star of all," Sabine continued, her voice barely a whisper; she edged closer so that their faces were only millimeters apart. "And it is rarely that its solstice aligns with the first full moon of the year. When this occurs, and a ceremony is held under its glow, it is said that any kind of magic can be fulfilled, for under the Star of Aramaar, our powers are raised to a level unparalleled in all of existence.

Of course, anyone who dares such a ritual must possess enough skill and power to control it," Sabine added, and her voice trembled as she spoke, "or face certain destruction."

Libby leaned as far back as possible.

"But if it's so dangerous, why would Zelna risk it?" she asked in one breath.

"Because if anyone has the power for such a feat, it is she," rasped Sabine, nodding her head with conviction. "And also, because I have reason to believe she had plans for this a long time ago," she stopped abruptly, as if once again censoring her thoughts, and then to Libby's immense relief, she shifted away so that she once more faced the fire. "In any case, it is near dawn and we have much to do. Are you up to the task, Liberty Frye?"

"Yes," said Libby, without even pausing to think. And then she remembered all of the bizarre things Sabine had just told her and suddenly felt a lot less confident. How was she supposed to go up against spells and witches and Solstices of … whatever it was?

"I was counting on that," Sabine whispered, her eyes growing strangely intense, and Libby noticed that her hands were now clasped tightly in her lap, perfectly still, but her body began to tremble ever so slightly. Several seconds ticked by and Sabine began to shake more and more until Libby wondered if she was having some sort of seizure.

"So … aren't you supposed to tell me what to do?"

"I almost dare not ask," Sabine eventually responded. "I almost do not trust myself, but I do not see another way!"

"Maybe if you just blurted it out?"

Sabine immediately stopped shaking. She blinked, straightened her posture, and turned to look Libby straight in the face. A look of clarity settled into her eyes. "Perhaps you are familiar with it," she began, and her voice was low, almost pleading. "The tree I spoke of earlier, Barvultmir? He produces volumes every year, enough to last until the next harvest."

Libby stared in utter despair at Sabine, not caring one microscopic spec what Barvultmir could or could not produce. "A tree?" she groaned, throwing her hands to her face. "That's your grand plan? To tell me about a *tree?*"

"Why, he's not just a tree. He's *your* tree. The descendant of Barvultmir, of course!"

Libby blinked, her mind swirling in confusion. "I'm sorry, but I ...."

"Think, Liberty Frye!" Sabine's fingers now dug into the sides of Libby's arms as she leaned toward her, her face wild with excitement. "Do you not know of it? Do you not have its fruit?"

"I-I don't know!" sputtered Libby, too terrified to even notice Sabine's toxic breath, for in truth, there isn't much in the world more frightening than being squeezed by an agitated witch. "Perhaps if you could—"

"I gave the last seed of Barvultmir to your mother; it was a parting gift—the last of the line of the Tree of Fire—and I have reason to believe she planted it. I have seen such news in the stars, and more than that, so much more than that, is the belief that everything hinges on, Liberty Frye!"

"What hinges on what?"

"I've told you, girl, the fruit!" cried Sabine. "Do you not have it? They are like berries, usually violet in color, and I was sure I read that they accompanied you here. Do you not have it somewhere … maybe a suitcase, some sort of carrying devise?"

"The purple berries," whispered Libby. "You're talking about those purple berries?"

"Yes! Surely, I did not read wrong?"

"I … I've got a few left in my backpack, I think, but it was left at my grandmother's house," grappled Libby, desperate to understand. "And-and you need them?"

Sabine fell back on her heels, as if exhausted from the sudden exertion. She stayed still until her rapid breathing slowly returned to normal, and when she raised her head to look at Libby once more, her expression had changed.

"*You* need the berries, Liberty Frye," she replied, and then she heaved herself back into her chair, taking a moment to get comfortable. "If you want to save your parents, you must bring those berries to me, whatever the cost."

14

Amulets and Fir Trees

The day arrived thick with fog. Libby rubbed her eyes, surprised to discover that she had fallen asleep, and for a brief moment, she was sure that the night before had all been a dream. And then, she saw Sabine standing before her, proudly presenting a breakfast of burnt toast and butter. Well, at least it wasn't blue, squiggly things, Libby noted with relief, and she sat up in her vegetable chair to eat as Sabine went over their plans once more.

By nine-forty, Libby found herself pedaling Sabine's rickety bicycle through the misty woods, and the air was so dense that it felt as if she was swimming through it rather than riding. A ratty coat from Sabine's closet hung down below her knees and the long scarf tied about her head billowed behind her like a flag as she pedaled faster and faster.

"It's a disguise," Sabine had explained while tucking a folded piece of paper into Libby's coat pocket. "If the raven is out, it will make you less recognizable."

Libby turned right at the path's intersection, just as Sabine had instructed, her lungs burning from the frosty air, and continued on, now heading toward a familiar, run-down house perched in front of a small clearing.

"Grandmother's," she muttered, pretending not to notice her thumping heart.

And then, she slowed down for a moment in confusion. Her chest felt ... *different*, as if her heart actually beat from the outside of her and was pulling away. She shook her head and glanced down at the watch Sabine had given her, forcing herself to concentrate. It was six minutes past ten. Her grandmother should be gone by now ....

The tugging in her chest grew stronger, pulling her toward the left-hand side of the trail, as if a gust of wind blew her that way. Libby pedaled harder against it, but then, a final thump of her chest yanked her sideways, knocking her off her bike, and she landed face-first inside the narrow ditch beside the pathway. She pushed herself up and immediately noticed that something was actually *poking out* from the center of her chest like an arrow! It tugged even harder to the left, forcing her to turn, and at the same time, she heard a muffled cough waft from somewhere in the trees.

"Who's there?" she wheezed, staggering against her will toward the sound.

"Libby?" came a hoarse response. "Libby, is that really you?"

Goosebumps washed over Libby's arms and legs as she tried to stop and look about her, but the tugging kept pulling her toward the voice. She lurched helplessly toward the sound, her chest yanking her harder and she was unable to stop herself now as she lunged between the trees, jerking absurdly like a puppet on strings—she was moving faster and faster, her legs barely able to keep up—she was stumbling toward the left, and now to the right, forward and then backwards—and then, she felt herself yanked sideways with so much force that she wondered if she had been caught up in some kind of invisible tornado … something dark zoomed toward her and she zoomed toward it … too late, she was going to hit it ….

When she opened her eyes, she found herself lying sideways on the ground, looking straight into a chubby, freckled face with big, brown eyes.

"*Ginny?*" Libby gasped.

Ginny only stared back at her with such a dumbstruck expression that, under any other circumstance, Libby would have burst out laughing.

"Ginny, what on earth are you doing here?" Libby cried between gulps of air, but something at her neck made it almost impossible to breathe. She struggled to free her arms, which was much more difficult than she anticipated, because the harder she tried to move away, the more Ginny crammed against her.

"Ginny, sorry, can you move a little?" grunted Libby, wiggling and squirming. "I think I'm stuck."

"C-can't move," was all that Ginny would say, her eyes wide and unblinking. And then she finally said something else that sounded like, "Necklace."

Libby continued to wiggle around until somehow, she managed to free her arms. She reached up and immediately felt the clasp of her necklace pressing into her throat, the chain cutting into her skin with so much force that she was sure it would slice right through her. She fumbled hurriedly with the chain, her fingers awkward from the cold, but she finally managed to slip it over her head, and then to her astonishment, the amulet popped out from under her clothes, zipped through the air and immediately clamped to the outside of Ginny's coat, the silver-colored chain clanging musically as it struck against itself in the process.

"What *is* that?" gasped Libby, scrambling to a sitting position.

Ginny blinked but said nothing.

"Ginny, are you okay? Say something! Anything!"

But Ginny remained on the ground, completely still, gaping back at her with the same, paralyzed expression. Several more seconds ticked by before Ginny struggled to a sitting position and looked around, a smattering of leaves and twigs sticking out from her hair in various directions.

"It ... it actually worked!" she blurted.

It took Ginny a while before she was able to speak in full sentences, but when she finally could, she talked so rapidly and with such increasing enthusiasm that Libby had a hard time keeping up. She told Libby all about running away and Uncle Frank and the necklaces and of Sal's plane ride across the world. Libby listened, completely stupefied, while Ginny told her about the landing and of her mad dash through the woods.

"... and then, just before the policeman was going to catch me, I lost my balance," continued Ginny, her eyes growing large at the memory. "I thought that was it for me, but just as I was blacking out, I got pulled out of the water!"

"By who?" gasped Libby.

"Some travelers, um, gypsies, really."

"*Gypsies?*"

Ginny nodded, staring distractedly at Libby's amulet that was still stuck to hers, and then she started, as if remembering something. She dug into her pocket and produced a sheer, metallic cloth satchel, identical to one Libby remembered seeing in the box when Uncle Frank had given her the necklace. With some difficulty, Ginny slipped the cloth over her pendant and immediately, the moonstones disengaged, sending Libby's necklace to the ground with a muted thump. They both stared at it for a moment.

"They were setting up camp and saw me as soon as I came out of the rapids," Ginny resumed excitedly, and from the expression on her face, it was clear that her story sounded as incredible to her as it did to Libby. "They fished me from the water and then I ... I convinced them to hide me," she added proudly. "I paid them of course—Uncle Frank gave me some money—and they took care of me until I was able to explain to them that I needed to come here."

Libby gaped at her friend in amazement. "And you did all of this for *me*?"

"I know," coughed Ginny, while nodding so enthusiastically that her cheeks shook a little. "I still can't believe it myself! I mean, I think I've just broken at least a hundred different rules, and you know what? I kind of like it!"

"Ginny, you are amazing!" wailed Libby, hugging her. "You're completely fantastic … you're the very best friend anyone could ever even imagine, but still, what were you thinking? You could have been *killed!*"

"Well, I almost was," agreed Ginny, clearly awed by the notion. "But that's the point; I thought there was no way I'd survive that fall, and now, look at me! Here I am, still alive, and I really did find you! I did it!"

"You did it!" laughed Libby, and Ginny's face beamed with the thrill of it all.

"I … I think I feel like a changed person," Ginny continued as if she were speaking and having an epiphany at the exact same time, and at this particular moment, she was just realizing the magnitude of her actions. "Like I could do almost anything, like I'm invincible! I want to keep doing things now, things that used to scare me—like eating escargot! Or no, something more than that, like, like, shooting those boys with a slingshot next time they try to push me around! I'll need to hone my hand-eye coordination skills, because I've never done anything athletic before, but you can help me with that, right?" She was saying all of this very quickly, and before Libby had a chance to realize she was being asked a question, Ginny continued, "I mean, if I can fly across the world and survive winter rapids and find you in the middle of the German woods, well," and she gasped at a sudden idea, "well, it's like it's my destiny to do the impossible!" she announced, and then she grabbed Libby by the shoulders, her eyes blazing with excitement. "Let's go find Sal, now; why not?!"

"Where is he?" stammered Libby, trying to mirror Ginny's enthusiasm, but in truth, she was beginning to feel slightly alarmed by it.

"I lost my radio in the river, so I have no idea," admitted Ginny, sobering a bit from the realization, but that only lasted a moment. "But it doesn't matter, anyhow, because now that I've found you, the hard part's over; we'll just head toward Hanau and once we find Sal, we'll radio Uncle Frank and figure out what to do from there!"

"Yes, but," Libby paused, feeling at a loss as to how to respond. Clearly, Ginny's enthusiasm had made her completely forget all about her parents, and Libby hadn't even begun to tell her all that had happened since their walkie-talkie call. But what was she supposed to say? Somehow, nothing she thought of sounded … well, not completely batty. "But do you know how to get to Hanau?"

It was the only thing Libby could think of.

"That's hardly the point!" answered Ginny. "Haven't you been listening at all?"

"Yes, of course, Ginny—but, now that you mention it, how did you find *me?*"

"All these questions," huffed Ginny, "are getting us nowhere!" But she fished begrudgingly into her pocket anyway and pulled out a tattered piece of paper. "Uncle Frank wrote down the address," she grumbled, and then nodded toward the house. "Besides, I'd recognize your backpack anywhere."

Libby followed Ginny's gaze, and from where she crouched, she could just make out an army green bag with distinctive, sew-on patches dangling from inside the attic windowpane. Something queasy rolled inside her stomach.

"What's the matter?" said Ginny.

Libby scurried toward some bushes, pulling Ginny along with her.

"Where are we going?"

"Just hide!" whispered Libby.

"Don't be silly," Ginny replied impatiently. "We don't need to hide; we need to figure out the way to Hanau. Besides, what are you afraid of? I'm invincible!"

"You may be invincible, Ginny, but you're not invisible," groaned Libby, "and right now, that's what we need."

Ginny looked a little deflated. "Well, I don't know how to do that yet."

"I was supposed to sneak into Grandmother's house after she left for her appointment in order to get my backpack."

"What for?"

Libby took a moment to compose her response, trying to

figure out a way to explain things so that Ginny would listen. "Because it has the Grimm Brothers book," she eventually replied, "and also, you know those berries I use for my slingshot?"

Ginny frowned, clearly annoyed by the tangent, but she nodded anyway.

"Well, Sabine says they've got some sort of power, and she needs them to make a potion—an antidote, I guess, and I'm supposed to bring my bag to her right away, but I can't! I mean, they've hung it there on purpose; they're trying to lure me! There's no way I can get up there now!"

Ginny fell into a spasm of coughs, but when she recovered, she asked, "Who's Sabine?"

Libby pressed her fingers to her forehead, trying to calm down. A thousand things popped into her head to say, but none of them sounded remotely sensible.

"I see your distress," Ginny remarked calmly. "For some reason, you can't go up there, but then, you don't have my experience. I'll do it!"

"I don't care how invincible you feel, Ginny, you are not going up there!" Libby hissed in exasperation. "It's too risky. We wouldn't stand a chance, trust me!"

"So, you think we need someone else's help?"

"There *is* no one else."

"Why not ask Wolfgang?"

Libby looked at her friend like she'd just turned into a purple chicken.

"Yeah," shrugged Ginny, "Wolfgang. Your parents' friend—the baker in town?"

"But how did you know …."

"Maybe *he* can get the bag for you."

It was the first time in the past hour that Ginny had said something lucid; even her expression was becoming less manic, almost as if she'd been knocked back to her senses. Libby was beginning to think that her friend had somehow traded her frenzied self-confidence in for some kind of psychic power when Ginny looked back at her sheepishly.

"I got Uncle Frank to tell me what he knew about your parents," she admitted. "He said Wolfgang was one of the only people they would ever talk about from their time here. It sounded like they were really close friends, so I just thought …."

"Ginny, you're a genius!" cried Libby.

"Well—"

"And I remember my parents mentioning that his shop was on the market square," Libby continued excitedly, and Ginny was nodding, "so we just need to make our way to Hanau!"

"Yes! Now, how do we do that?"

"But I thought you said you could find it!"

"That was just a momentary exhilaration," replied Ginny. "I'm starting to feel much better now, thank goodness. What are you doing?"

Libby didn't respond because she was fumbling inside her enormous coat for something. She pulled out what looked like a dried sea slug and flung it away in disgust, reaching into her coat again, this time pulling out a piece of folded paper.

"I almost forgot about Sabine's directions—I think it's

some sort of map," she explained excitedly. "She said it would help me if I needed to find my way." She smoothed the paper over the ground, only to discover that it was completely blank, with the exception of five words:

ASK THE TREES FOR HELP

Libby blinked, read it again, and moaned.

"What's it supposed to *mean?*" Ginny murmured.

Libby stuffed the paper back into her coat and threw up her arms in frustration. "The entire world has gone mental!"

"Maybe it's a riddle!" continued Ginny. "Let me think; what's like a tree, but isn't?"

Something in Libby snapped.

"No, Ginny, it means I'm just supposed to turn to a tree like this one," she said, her voice growing high-pitched, and Ginny tried to signal for her to be quiet, but Libby only giggled manically while bowing to a very old, very tall evergreen. "And say, 'Hey, Mister Tree, so sorry to bother you on such a fine winter morning, but could you please point me the way to the Hanau marketplace?'" Libby giggled harder, unable to stop herself, waving her arms and gesturing wildly, until she suddenly collapsed in exhaustion, too miserable to care that she had landed in a slushy puddle of mud.

"Libby!" Ginny called in alarm.

"It's no use," Libby wailed. "I don't know what I'm doing anymore—I don't even know *who I am* anymore! And-and worse than that," she hiccupped, "I don't know what's *real* anymore! I mean, look at this! Look at me!" she blubbered, glancing up at Ginny with a muddy face. "My parents may or may not be waiting on my help—I don't even know—and here I am, without any way to reach them, and now I've dragged you into it, and-and all I've got are instructions from some crazy old lady to talk to a *freaking tree!*"

"But ... it's pointing."

"What?" sobbed Libby, looking blearily up at her friend, but Ginny's eyes were glued to the evergreen, and her face was as white as confectioner's sugar, and she stood perfectly still, one hand lifted in the direction of the tree in front of them.

"The tree ... um, it ... it's *pointing*," Ginny repeated, her hand still frozen in the air. "I saw it, Libby! It moved!"

And indeed, the tree *was* pointing, and it was a very strange sight to see an enormous, shaggy evergreen bent halfway down so that it formed a perfect arrow, pointing with the top half of its limbs toward the north end of the bicycle bath.

Libby wiped the mud from her eyes and blinked in astonishment. "Thank you," she whispered.

The tree wiggled its tip, as if nodding in acknowledgment, and then it went back into the arrow shape. Ginny continued to stare at it as Libby scrambled to her feet.

"Ginny," she said hoarsely, "it looks like we're going to Hanau!"

15

ᴄWOLFGANG'S ᴮBÄCKEREI

G inny didn't respond because she was too busy gawking at the tree, and then she was being tugged by Libby towards the bicycle.

"Get on," Libby said. "And hold on tight. The path's a bit bumpy in places."

Ginny blinked.

"Hurry, Ginny!"

Ginny stumbled onto the bicycle, trying her best to situate herself on the uncomfortable luggage rack while glancing repeatedly back at the tree that was now in the process of straightening itself—and it seemed as though that grand, old evergreen might have a bit of a stiff back—and then, they were off, speeding down the path in the direction that the tree had pointed.

When they had traveled a safe distance from the house, Ginny lifted her head and shouted, "Could you please explain why a tree just gave us directions?"

Libby kept pedaling, glancing uneasily about her as they passed through an area with nothing to shelter them from view, but she was relieved to see no sign of the raven. The sky was now patched with blue and Libby wondered how far away the marketplace would be, and what she would say to this Wolfgang when—and if—she found him. Should she just announce herself? Would he know who she was? Or worse, what if he couldn't help her, and then she'd have no way to get those berries out of the house ....

"Seriously," Ginny was saying, "didn't you see that tree pointing? I know I saw that tree pointing! And I'm not crazy! Admit it! You saw a huge pine tree pointing!"

"I saw it," said Libby, and she pedaled faster, heading toward the bend where the trees once more shadowed their path, and a feeling of dread settled into her stomach. What if she was too late? What if her parents couldn't really be helped? What if Zelna had changed plans somehow and now she wouldn't be able to find them? And what about the berries? she worried again. She had to get those berries....

"You asked for the tree to point, and it bent down and made a huge arrow," Ginny continued from behind her. "Admit it! You talked to a tree and it did exactly what you asked! I saw it!"

"Yes, I talked to the tree and then the tree pointed," panted Libby, who was getting rather tired. After all, it was hard enough pedaling a rickety bicycle through the woods for several kilometers, but Ginny wasn't exactly a light load, and this ridiculous disguise she was wearing didn't make things any easier.

"How can you say that?" demanded Ginny, her voice growing slightly hysterical. "How can you sit there and tell me that you asked a tree for directions, and then it bent down and pointed for you? It's impossible! I'm not crazy, you know!"

"I know you're not crazy," wheezed Libby, her face beading with sweat.

"Then you'd better tell me what's going on!" Ginny practically screamed. "How come I just saw what I saw, and what I saw was *you* talking to a tree?"

"Because." Libby strained to get up a hill. "Apparently …." She stopped at the top and panted harder, letting herself think for a moment. "Well, put it this way," she continued, now gliding down the path, "know how Julie Lambert thinks I'm a freak of nature?"

"That has nothing to do with a tree."

"But it does, actually," said Libby, realizing it for the first time herself. "Remember how, in science class, when we're going to do an experiment, and then all of the sudden, the Bunsen burner on our table turns on all by itself?" Libby asked very slowly, thinking it through as she spoke; in fact, Libby considered, a lot of things made sense that hadn't before. Ridiculous things that only happened to her….

"A tree just *pointed* for you, and you're talking to me about science experiments?"

"Or, when we're about to watch a movie in class," continued Libby, deep in thought, "and then, even though Ms. Fisher likes to keep the lights on, they go off anyway?"

"Why do you keep changing the subject?"

"Or when I think about things sometimes—like the time when Bobbie Johnson got in front of the whole class and called you … something mean," Libby paused.

"He called me fat," snapped Ginny.

"Okay, well, remember how I said I ought to punch him in the eye for being so rude, and you told me not to because it would just make things worse so I didn't, but then, the next day, he showed up at school with a black eye?"

"Coincidence," sniffed Ginny with a hint of satisfaction in her voice. "He said a coconut fell off a delivery truck outside the Piggly Wiggly."

"When have you ever seen a coconut being sold at the Piggly Wiggly?"

"Never … but I've never really looked, either."

"And it just happens to hit him in the exact spot I was thinking of during the same time frame that I was thinking about it?"

"Well, it did."

Libby continued pedaling until she reached a crossroads. A small wooden post with two signs pointed left to Hanau and right to Erlensee. Libby turned left, now following a widening stream that cut through the woods.

"You could be right, it could be coincidence that I think things and then they just sort of happen," admitted Libby, not quite believing what she was about to say, "or it could be because … apparently … accordingly to someone at least, and this is going to sound truly insane …."

"*WHAT?*"

"Well, I'm a witch," Libby finished very quickly.

"A witch," repeated Ginny.

"Um … yes," grimaced Libby, and she thought how strange it was to actually say that out loud. "Or at least, according to Sabine, I've got it in my blood or something, and that's why the trees can communicate with me—"

"Because you're a *witch.*"

"And it's got something to do with why my parents were poisoned and why I was kidnapped," continued Libby, the words now rushing out of her. "And there's some Solstice of Arama or Aramor or something or other tonight where there will be a ceremony and Zelna has something terrible planned, which is why I've got to bring the berries of Barvultmir back to Sabine before then so she can create an antidote for my parents!"

"A witch—wait, you're parents are still *alive?*"

"But we've got to be very careful not to be seen because Iorgu will be looking for me. And I already know from the fact that my bag was hanging from the window that they know I've escaped! I don't know how much time we've got before …."

The sound of rushing wings caught Libby's breath and her skin prickled instinctively. She craned to look over her shoulder, but all she could see was Ginny glaring back at her.

"Ginny," she choked, now pedaling with all of her might, because the sound of the wings grew closer, and she felt that terrible clutch on her heart, like she used to have when she was little and would have dreams about a giant chasing her up a hill, and she knew that, any minute, that giant would catch her, but she didn't dare look backwards; she had to keep going. "It's a raven, isn't it?"

"Ho-ly Mac-a-ro-ni," Ginny wheezed, her voice barely a whisper.

"He's close, isn't he?" Libby panted, terror pushing at her temples now so that her head throbbed with her heart, but Ginny just made a funny noise that sounded something like:

"Haouewww."

"Is ... is there one or two of them?" gasped Libby, but then, before Ginny could answer, something brushed over her head, and in the next instant, she was breaking to a stop with all of her might, Sabine's rusty bicycle shrieking in protest as Libby pressed in the hand brake and slammed the pedals backwards.

"Whaaa," came Ginny's voice.

Libby leapt from the bike, barely holding it steady long enough for Ginny to tumble off, and she stared in absolute, complete disbelief at what had landed on the path directly in front of them.

"It's—it's Buttercup!" wheezed Ginny.

And it *was* Buttercup, no matter how impossible it seemed; Libby would have recognized him anywhere, even though his chain of purple berries was conspicuously missing. She ran over to him, scooping him into her arms, and not a minute too soon, because he collapsed immediately in exhaustion, his white head falling limply over her shoulder.

"He … he followed you across the *world*," murmured Ginny in amazement, and for just a moment, she seemed to have forgotten all about their conversation, specifically the part where her best friend had just finished telling her that she was a witch.

Libby nodded, and it felt like a humungous apple had bobbed into her throat. She kissed the top of Buttercup's head, holding him close, her throat too tight to speak, but Buttercup didn't care about all the fuss he'd caused; he was already fast asleep, his breathing deep and slow. Libby wondered if he had slept or eaten at all in the past week. Gingerly, she handed him over to Ginny and then picked up the bicycle.

"We've got to get him someplace to rest," she managed to say, wiping her eyes while pointing to a sign fifteen feet down the path. "I think we're nearly there; we'll take him to Wolfgang's."

When they reached the cobblestone square of the marketplace, it was abuzz with activity. White tents popped up everywhere, selling things that smelled and looked delicious.

There was a stand selling *Shneeballen*, which were clusters of candy covered, funnel-cake-like balls, so big one would have to hold them in both hands, and *Glühwein* that steamed in brown ceramic mugs and smelled just like hot, spiced apple cider, and *Pommes Frites* that, Libby could tell by looking at them, were freshly made French fries piled high inside paper cones and sold with a side of mayonnaise. Her stomach growled noisily.

"Oh, this is torture," moaned Ginny, still carrying Buttercup in her arms.

Libby steered their bike between the stalls, overcome by the smells and chatter and the bustle of people everywhere, and she tried her best to ignore the cart steaming with cooked bratwursts and sauerkraut—just like her mom would make— that they were now walking past. An accordion player pulled up a stool beside the cart and began playing a song, and despite her aching stomach, Libby couldn't help but smile. Now *this*, she thought to herself, is Germany.

"Hey, I saw that on the Hanau webpage!" called Ginny, pointing to a statue toward the end of the square. "It's the Grimm Brothers! I think Hanau was their birthplace or something."

Libby looked up, relieved to be distracted from the food, and saw a bronze statue of two men towering before them. It was an odd moment, and as she gazed into the larger-than-life faces of Jacob and Wilhelm Grimm, she felt like she was meeting two people whom she already knew.

Just then, Buttercup started from his slumbers, lifting his head with a jerk and looking around in a funny sort of way.

"Maybe you can ask them for directions to Wolfgang's," suggested Ginny as she motioned toward the statue. She leaned in and whispered, "You know, like you did before?"

"I think it has to be a tree," said Libby, glancing uneasily at Buttercup. He was growing into a peculiar shade of blue.

"We've got to get him somewhere fast—he looks really sick. Help me look for the bakery, Ginny. Here, I'll take Buttercup; you take the bike. If Wolfgang's still in business, his shop should be right off the square somewhere."

Ginny looked disappointed, but she turned around and headed toward the far left side of the market, pushing Sabine's creaky bicycle by her side. Libby headed toward the right, now with Buttercup in her arms, barely able to squeeze between the increasing crowds.

She looked in dismay about her; on all sides of the square, shops crammed into every spare inch of space, practically toppling over each other, all with names like *Schlächterei* or *Stationäres Geschäft*.

"How am I supposed to know where Wolfgang's bakery is in all of this?" Libby murmured, glancing anxiously down at Buttercup, but when she did, she almost dropped him in surprise, because he had one very unnatural, blue-hued wing lifted up, and Libby could have sworn that the tips of his feathers were forming into a shape similar to a pointed finger, which was indicating a row of shops directly to her left.

"Buttercup, are you telling me where the bakery is?" gasped Libby, but Buttercup only made a sound that sounded a bit like a burp, and then he dropped his head on her shoulder once more.

"Ginny!" Libby called, running to get her, which didn't take very much effort because she found her standing at a stall only thirty feet away, blissfully sampling a variety of confections.

"Ginny, quick! I think Buttercup just pointed!"

Ginny was in the process of popping a chocolate cashew into her mouth, and she looked up in surprise, her eyes wide with guilt.

"Ewas jus so hungry," she gulped through her mouthful, "an' ther fwee samples an' so delicious …."

"Never mind that, let's go," said Libby, tugging her away from the stall, and Ginny threw a forlorn glance at the remaining samples while she stumbled along with the bike.

The woman at the stall wasn't at all sorry to see her go, muttering something disapproving under her breath that sounded a lot like, "Amerikanisch tourist."

"This way, I think," called Libby.

And sure enough, as soon as they crossed to the other side of the square, Libby spotted a narrow shop with an enormous pretzel hanging from the door awning. A painted, wooden sign just beside it said:

"Bäckerei Wolfgang."

Ginny parked their bicycle against the shop wall, her eyes never leaving the giant pretzel, while Libby opened the shop door with her free hand.

A small bell tinkled merrily as she stepped inside and she noticed four cute little tables nestled along the edge of the wall, complete with dainty wooden chairs, checkered red tablecloths and colorful vases filled with pretty little daisies. Across the room, a wide, glass counter loomed before them, filled with a mouth-watering assortment of baked goods: apple pies, cheesecakes, croissants, chocolate rolls, cheese sticks, pretzels ….

Libby's stomach growled again. Somewhere behind her, Ginny moaned.

"Guten Tag!" boomed a voice, and a robust, elderly man popped up from behind the counter, his red, round face dusted with flour, as were the tips of his giant mustaches. The man wiped his hands on the white apron that stretched across his ample stomach, and then he pushed back the tip of his baker's cap that had flopped over an eye.

"Er, Guten Tag," Libby repeated uncertainly. "Um, Sprechen Sie English?"

The man raised his eyebrows, and Libby had the horrible feeling that somehow, she'd just insulted him.

"Sprechen Sie *English*?" he repeated with great dignity, waving a pastry liner in the air. "Ich spreche Deutsch! Je parle Français! Parlo Italiano!" he bellowed, his enormous mustaches moving stiffly with each syllable—and really, it was quite distracting. "Am I not an internationally known baker? Of course I speak English!"

"That's *four languages!*" gulped Ginny, forgetting all about the giant pretzel. "I've never met anyone who could speak four languages!"

"You must be American."

"Yes, sir," replied Libby, feeling rather intimidated, "and ... well, excuse me for having to ask this, but you are Wolfgang, right?"

The man studied her for a moment, sizing up her unusual attire, and then he glanced between Ginny and Buttercup, who was at this particular moment making strange, gurgling noises in his sleep.

"I take it you are not here for my fine baked goods," he sighed.

"I'll handle this," said Ginny, and before Libby could stop her, she was marching right up to the baker, producing a small wad of dollar bills from her pocket in the process. She counted out three and carefully placed them on the counter top. "We'll take one of everything," she announced loudly, the way people do when they are speaking to foreigners because, for whatever reason, it seems a generally accepted fact that speaking louder makes a person understand them better.

Libby groaned and put her head against Buttercup, but just then—and she didn't know if it was a good sign or a bad one—the baker burst out laughing.

"Meine Güte! One of everydhing, widh dhree American dollars!"

Ginny's face turned red.

"Well, I only have ten bucks left," she replied a bit huffily, "and I thought I'd have to buy stuff before you'd talk to us."

Something she said must have struck him, because he immediately stopped laughing.

"You have a very blue goose," he frowned.

"He's sick," said Libby, and Wolfgang nodded slowly in agreement.

"May I inquire why two young ladies widh a sick goose are looking for me?"

Libby gulped, suddenly feeling rather panicky. What should she say to him? She hadn't really had a chance to think it all through. She couldn't just show up at his bakery, with no identification or any other way to prove to him who she really was, and tell him everything that had happened—he'd think she was crazy!

"Of course," sniffed Ginny, and Libby breathed a sigh of relief that she was taking it over. "We'll be happy to explain exactly why we're here … Libby, you tell him."

Libby gulped again, looking from Ginny to an increasingly impatient baker with twitching mustaches, and then she stepped forward and said the first thing that came to her mind:

"I'm the daughter of Peter and Gretchen Frye." She could tell by the sudden O-shape of his mouth that this was not the response he had been expecting. "My parents are in terrible danger and we've-we've, well sir, we've come for your help!"

16

The Cycle of Sicherheit

Wolfgang walked straight over to the door, locked it, and then flipped a white sign that hung from a peg above the window that said "Geschlossen" in bright red letters. He closed the window curtains and switched off the lights. When he turned around, Libby could see that he had turned very pale.

"Who sent you?"

"No one," stammered Libby, "I mean, we just thought ...."

"But how did you know?"

"Know what?"

"About *me!*"

"Oh, well my parents mentioned that they wanted to visit you," said Libby, trying her best to explain things. "And then

Ginny found out about you from my Uncle Frank, see, and when we couldn't get my bag back from my grandmother's house, we were hoping you could help—"

"Impossible!" Wolfgang bellowed, pacing the floor. He suddenly turned to her, looking down at her for a long, silent minute. "But I recognize you," he finally said, and then he marched across the room, squeezed back behind the counter and disappeared through a door.

Libby and Ginny glanced at each other.

"Well, that went well."

"Three dollars should have bought *something*," muttered Ginny, staring rather passionately at a strawberry cupcake on the second shelf of the glass display. "Those chocolates outside were the first thing I've had to eat in *two days*."

Buttercup burped in his sleep, and even in the darkness of the shuttered bakery, Libby could tell that he was turning into an alarming shade of violet. In fact, his color bore an uncanny resemblance to the berries that were missing from around his neck, and it dawned on her that he just might have eaten them; after all, he'd flown across the Atlantic, hadn't he? He must have survived off *something*.

She glanced worriedly from Buttercup to the doorway, just as Wolfgang returned through it, carrying a scrapbook under his arm.

"Full name," he demanded, slamming the book onto one of the tables.

"Um, Liberty—Liberty Francis Frye," Libby sputtered in alarm.

"*Francis!*" giggled Ginny, but Libby glared back at her.

"Root name!" barked Wolfgang.

"Tuber," blurted Libby, which confused her at first, until she remembered a game she and her mother used to play when she was much younger ….

"Code name!" Wolfgang roared, and at this point, he looked so agitated that Libby wasn't sure if she should say anything at all, but still, she couldn't help herself, because without even thinking, she shouted out:

"Sassafras!"

At this, Wolfgang drew back. He frowned. He scratched his chin. He placed his wide hand on his left hip and looked down at the floor, all the while shaking his head. And then he muttered, "I was sure she would've picked Julep."

"Julep!" Libby said, remembering it, too. "Yes, she would say that! She would say something about her friend who would expect Julep, but for me, it was always Sassafras."

Wolfgang inhaled sharply through his nose.

"Makes sense," he mumbled begrudgingly, and then he pointed to the scrapbook on the table. "I've been keeping up widh you. I'll get you some tea and pastries."

He left again; Libby and Ginny threw another glance at each other and then walked over to the table where Wolfgang had left the scrapbook.

Libby opened the cover.

"That's my mom," she said, recognizing her immediately, even though her hair was dyed a strange color of red. She was standing in the bakery next to Wolfgang, wearing a white apron and white hat, holding a certificate, and laughing at something Libby couldn't see.

"Bäckereigeselle Tag" was written directly underneath.

"Look at this," said Ginny, pointing to the opposite page, and Libby turned to a picture of her mother in a formal black silk dress, her dark hair tumbling over her shoulders, and her father standing in full military uniform.

"Dheir wedding day," said Wolfgang, setting a tray in front of them. He picked up a bowl and put it down beside Buttercup. "Dhey had dhat taken in Rothenburg ob der Tauber—where dhey were married."

"She's in black," said Libby.

"Dhat's Gretchen for you," sighed Wolfgang. "She marched to her own beat, I denk is dhe saying? I tried to get her a white dress, but she wouldn't have it. She said dhis was her favorite, and a favorite dress was more important dhan a color," he chuckled sadly, and his eyes glistened with sudden tears. "She was like a daughter to me."

Libby turned the page, and this time, a letter was taped to it, and she recognized her father's handwriting.

"Grand Rapids, Michigan?" murmured Libby, staring at the postal address.

Wolfgang raised his eyebrows as he sipped a cup of tea. "Peter always mailed me dheir letters whenever he was on a business trip," he explained.

"Why?"

"Grundgütiger! Don't you know?"

Libby shook her head.

"Dhey were protecting you, Libby! Dhey gave up everydhing for you!"

Chapter 16

"Protecting me from what?" she asked, and Wolfgang's eyes bulged out like he'd just choked on something. Slowly, he sat down, his wide frame dwarfing the little shop chair.

"I was your Mutter's closest friend," he slowly replied, "and she told me dhings in confidence she'd never told anyone before. But even so, I had assumed you were aware!"

"Sabine already told me that she was studying to be a witch, if that's what you mean—"

A mouthful of tea suddenly sprayed her from the side.

"Sorry," hiccupped Ginny, mopping at Libby's arm.

"And did Sabine tell you her role in it all?" Wolfgang growled.

"Well, no," gulped Libby, confused by his sudden temper. "I mean, yes, she said that she was the one who taught her …."

"And dhe one who betrayed her, too," Wolfgang spat out in disgust. "Dhe one who set her up, who nearly had her killed on dhe day of her wedding, and all for what? Money!" he roared, slamming his fist down on the table, and his outrage terrified Libby so much that she felt glued to her seat—she couldn't have run away if she'd wanted. "Jealousy! Laziness! Your Mutter's a verdammt saint in dhe midst of Teufels!"

Libby didn't know what a Teufel was, but all the same, she knew that it must be pretty bad, because Wolfgang's face was positively livid. She picked up her cup of tea and tried to take a sip, but her hands were shaking, which made it difficult to look casual. On the bright side, Ginny had recovered from her initial shock, and was now blissfully enjoying a cream cheese danish.

"She never even knew about it until it was too late," he choked out angrily, and then he took another deep breath through his nose, closing his eyes for a moment, and he continued to breathe in and out, until he looked considerably calmer.

"I forget myself," he muttered, glancing apologetically over at Libby. "Dhis is not dhe time to relive what cannot be undone. Please, tell me what has happened. I need to know dhat first, dhen I'll decide."

And so, as soon as she was able to recover her speech, Libby told him, starting with the yellow envelope and ending with his bakery, and even Ginny stopped eating midway through it, her hand frozen halfway between her mouth and the plate of pastries, as she listened, round-eyed as Libby told them about the black cauldron, and then of Emil's rescue from the castle tower and finally, of her encounter with Sabine. When she had finished, Wolfgang looked surprisingly unfazed; Ginny, on the other hand, was not.

"I thought you were messing with me about the witch thing," she gasped. "I mean, the tree, well, that was weird, but I didn't think …." She stopped, grabbed her teacup and gulped down its contents in one long swallow. "I think I need some more of this," she whispered, and Wolfgang immediately rose from the table.

"I tried to tell you," muttered Libby, but Ginny merely blinked, saying nothing. Several seconds ticked by. From Libby's side of the table, Buttercup's snores could be heard. He must have been having a dream, because he kept twitching in a peculiar sort of way and Libby couldn't be sure, but it looked like something in his neck was wriggling.

"Chamomile, should be calming," announced Wolfgang, returning with another steaming cup. He set it in front of Ginny, and then he chuckled softly to himself as he took a seat, glancing over at Libby. "Your Mutter, now she knew how to make some tea! Dhat girl used herbs I'd never heard of, but, jawohl! did dhey work! Got me off dhe hard stuff ... well, most of dhe time," and then he grew serious once more, frowning down at the table top. When he spoke again, his words were measured, as if he were considering each and every syllable.

"You know about Zelna, about Sabine, about me," he resumed, looking thoughtfully into Libby's face.

"Yes ... well, sort of," she whispered.

"Your Mutter was never even dhat lucky. She was kept in dhe dark her whole life; Giselle wanted nodhing to do widh dhe Coven of Hessen. She despised it as much as she resented Zelna, and was determined dhat Gretchen should never learn of her bloodline. It was by mistake dhat she did, or radher, because of Sabine ...." He trailed off, sorting once again through his words. "It was not until Gretchen was much older dhat she learned dhe trudh," he resumed. "It was under Sabine's encouragement dhat she also took it up, learning what she called 'dhe healing disciplines,' denking dhese were dhings dhat could lead to no harm, and of course, Sabine taught dhem to her gladly, flattered to have such a distinguished protégé, and not once considering dhe price Gretchen would have to pay."

"What do you mean?"

Wolfgang shifted in his tiny seat, and then pointed a large forefinger down at the scrapbook. "I mean dhat because of dhis learning, Gretchen's whole life changed, and dhe lives of dhose connected to her, forever. I mean dhat, if Sabine had minded her own business, my best friend and your Vater might still be here, happily raising you dhe way Gretchen always dreamed, instead of living in ... in, well ...." He shrugged.

"Instead of living in Mississippi?"

"Well, it's no Dusseldorf."

Libby decided to let that go for the sake of progress.

"Why couldn't they have lived in Germany if they wanted?" she asked, but Wolfgang didn't answer at first. He emptied his cup as he turned several pages of the scrapbook, each with letters pinned to them, addressed from places like Stockton, California; or San Antonio, Texas; or Boston, Massachusetts. "I didn't know my dad went on so many business trips," Libby murmured, gazing dazedly at the addresses flashing by.

"Ten years is a long time," Wolfgang reminded her, and then he stopped at a page with a picture of Libby and her parents, with another letter pinned beside it, dated in August of that year, and posted from New Orleans, Louisiana.

"Well, that's *much* closer to home."

"It was dhe first time your Mutter sent me a picture since dhey left," said Wolfgang, nodding toward the page, and Libby noticed that he used his mustaches like pointers, tilting them this way and that to indicate the appropriate direction. In a weird way, it was actually pretty fascinating, and it seemed that the more interested he became in something, the more those giant mustaches would twitch.

"She was so happy; in her letter, she was positively gebegeistert!" he exclaimed. Before Libby had a chance to ask what that meant, Wolfgang was leaning toward her, his small, grey eyes shining with intensity, and his voice was strangely contained. "Did she say anydhing unusual to you about dhat day, Libby?" he asked, pointing once again to the picture. "Do you remember anydhing out of dhe ordinary?"

"Well, it was my birthday," said Libby, quickly looking back down at the photo because Wolfgang's twitching mustaches made it impossible for her to concentrate.

She continued to stare at the picture, trying to recall the details, and she smiled, remembering when Uncle Frank had taken it of them—they'd gone to the reservoir for the day to go swimming, and Uncle Frank had spent the whole afternoon on the shore, snapping photos and yelling theories to them from his mobile unit, until a disgruntled woman waddled out of the lake and loudly informed him that no one cared about the possibilities of teleportation, to which he replied by calling her a fussocky ninnyhammer and was promptly asked to leave by park security for using foul language in a family zone—and then she began to remember little things her parents had said that day, strange remarks that she hadn't really paid much attention to at the time ....

"Somedhing about your age, perhaps?" prompted Wolfgang.

"She said this year was extra special," remembered Libby,

tracing around her mother's laughing face. "That I had just completed the most important cycle of growth."

"And entered dhe Cycle of Sicherheit?"

"Yes!" gasped Libby, looking up from the photo. "She said that I had passed into safety, or something like that. I thought it was just one of her random sayings," she looked back at Wolfgang, who was watching her very closely, his mustaches wriggling away. "What do you think—" She stopped, because suddenly, she knew: "She was *waiting* for me to turn ten, wasn't she?"

Wolfgang nodded slowly.

"But why?"

"No idea. Sabine should have been able to tell you *dhat,*" he grumbled, "but she didn't mention it, did she?"

Libby shook her head.

"She will when I get to her," he muttered darkly, looking away. He frowned down at the tabletop for several more seconds before resuming. "When your parents got married, it triggered two dhings: somedhing your grandmutter Giselle wanted to prevent and somedhing dhat Zelna wanted to destroy ... do you know what dhose might be?"

Libby threw Ginny a bewildered look, but Ginny was staring at something on the floor, so Libby took a guess: "Unwanted guests?"

Wolfgang snorted. "Dhere were no guests—dhey eloped. No, denken, Libby. You said dhat you found your grandmutter in dhe attic when you awoke dhat day, after you dhought your parents were dead."

"Yes," murmured Libby.

"And what did you find dhere, besides your book?"

"My grandfather's will," she replied, and for some reason she didn't understand, Ginny made a funny noise that sounded like a mix between a snort and a gasp.

"Leaving his fortune to you, yes?"

"I ... I think so," she answered, trying to remember, but it had seemed relatively insignificant compared to everything else at the time, and the memory was hazy, like she was trying to recall a dream. "I mean, it wasn't exactly in those words; it said something about a key, I think, something about a key in my book."

"And now, Sabine has risked *your* life to send you after it," snarled Wolfgang. "Why do you dhink she would do dhat?"

"She said she had to have it—the book and the berries," stammered Libby, who was getting worried, because everything she said just made Wolfgang more agitated, which, really, was the opposite of what she had hoped to achieve.

"No, oh, no," whispered Ginny.

"What for?" growled Wolfgang.

"I already told you," Libby replied nervously. "To ... to make some kind of antidote that will save my parents."

"Dhat's dhe Beeren," snapped Wolfgang, his mustaches twitching wildly, and his forehead began to grow pink. "But what about dhe book? Why do you denk she wants you to get *dhat?*"

Libby pressed her fingertips to her temples, suddenly feeling extremely overwhelmed, and it was difficult to think with all the scuffling going on beside her. "I don't know exactly," she blurted. "She said she'd explain it when I brought her the backpack—" and then she stopped speaking because Wolfgang's entire face flushed into a deep shade of red.

"I'll *bet* she will!" he practically hissed, his eyes narrowing in anger, and then his gaze shifted downward in surprise, just as Buttercup let out a long, loud burp.

"Something awful is happening!" Ginny wailed.

Libby scrambled from her chair, certain she was seeing things, but if she was, then Ginny was, too, because now they were both crouched on the floor, staring at a violet-hued, convulsing Buttercup, who was somehow still fast asleep, but that wasn't the alarming part. The alarming part was that a green sprig of tree was growing right out of Buttercup's snoring mouth, inching taller by the minute.

"He's *sprouting*," sobbed Ginny, and Libby bent herself over Buttercup, too horrified to speak for several seconds. Wolfgang leapt from the table, his face coloring all the more at the sight of him.

"Himmelherrgott!"

"Sabine!" wheezed Libby.

"You denk she did this?"

"Why would anyone do such a thing?" bawled Ginny.

"No, of course not … it's the berries, I'm sure of it!"

"Dhe Beeren?"

"There's no time to explain," said Libby, trying not to freak out completely, which is a lot harder to achieve with a blooming goose in one's arms, "we need a car … Wolfgang, can you take us to Sabine?"

But Wolfgang was already throwing on his coat without even changing out of his apron.

"Widh pleasure," he growled, slinging open the door.

17

THE FRUIT OF BARVULTMIR

By the time they reached the abbey ruins, Wolfgang's face was no longer red. It was purple. In fact, he almost matched Buttercup, who convulsed and burped so violently that Libby was in tears, feeling utterly helpless to do anything but watch. Even so, she was glad they were back at the abbey—even if Wolfgang was in an exceedingly vile temper—because if anyone could help Buttercup, it was Sabine.

Wolfgang marched out of his tiny car, lifted Buttercup into his arms and stalked over the large boulders surrounding Sabine's hut, not even pausing at the front door to knock—he simply barged in.

"You Weibsbild!" he roared as Libby and Ginny stumbled in after him.

"You said this lady's a witch, right?" Ginny gulped, looking around at the bizarre decor, and Libby nodded uneasily. "Then I wish he'd be polite, at least—even I know you're not supposed to tick off a witch!"

"I know you're in there, you Schlingel! Come out and show yourself!"

"Schlingel?" worried Ginny under her breath. "I don't know what that is, but it sounds like an insult, doesn't it sound like an insult to you?"

Libby wasn't listening, because she was busy clearing a space for Buttercup on Sabine's cluttered table, lifting containers of shriveled fish fins and pickled lizard tongue out of the way. She grabbed a jar filled with some sort of gelatinous substance and handed it off to Ginny.

"Oh, *gross!*" squealed Ginny, gawking at the label. "Hippo Earwax?"

"Was ist es jetzt?" screamed a voice from the front door. They all turned to see Sabine shuffle through it, holding a basket full of lichens and mushrooms, and then she nearly dropped it on the floor. "Huch!" she gasped. "I thought you were ... someone else."

"Sabine, please help!" wailed Libby, tugging Wolfgang toward the table so she could get Buttercup placed on it. "It's my pet—he's—he's," she paused, not knowing exactly *how* to describe it, but as soon as Sabine caught sight of him, she was running—well, it was more like hobbling, really—over to them.

"Stout girl, hold my fungus," she commanded, slinging her basket at Ginny, and then she grabbed Buttercup from

Wolfgang's arms and placed him on the table, bending her ugly face over him, turning his head this way and that. "Let me see, yes, yes, but what have we here!" she wheezed excitedly. "Chestnut stem properties, heart-shaped leaves, spiral grain pattern, a kink in the first twig ... by the hairy roots of Barvultmir, Liberty Frye, come here quickly, girl, now—is that what I think it is?"

"If you mean the berries, then, yes, I think so," gulped Libby, wiping tears from her eyes. "Can you save him, Sabine?"

Sabine didn't respond. Instead, she bent her head even lower over Buttercup, staring into his open bill for a full two minutes, and it was all Libby could do not to scream at her to hurry. Finally, Sabine sighed heavily and then glanced back up, her face filled with disappointment—disgust, even.

"It'll die," she pronounced flatly.

"What?" gasped Ginny.

"What do you mean, he'll die?" panicked Libby. "Can't you *do* something?"

"Not him ... it," sniffed Sabine, pointing a rather dirty finger at the tree. "It is already fading, don't you see the withering tips? Classic sign of pre-cognitive submission. Your goose, on the other hand, will be fine."

Libby blinked in confusion at the tree, not knowing what to make of what Sabine had just said, but then again, she *did* notice that the tiny branches were curling back, and more than that, the trunk was slowly deflating, until the little shoot flopped in half, now hanging limply out of Buttercup's snoring mouth.

"It didn't stand a chance," muttered Sabine, glumly plucking the dead tree and flinging it to the floor.

"He'll be alright? You're sure?" pressed Libby, watching Buttercup as he shifted in his sleep. "He still looks … purple."

"Serves him right. Tell me," she demanded, pointing a bony finger down at Buttercup. "How did he manage to obtain that seed?"

"I had a necklace I'd made for him …."

"From the tree?" breathed Sabine. *"A whole necklace?"*

"Yes—he must have eaten it on the way," stammered Libby, feeling confused by Sabine's behavior, but then she lost her train of thought because as soon as she said this, Sabine nearly knocked her over as she leapt toward a large book sitting on the kitchen counter. Sabine thumbed frenetically through it, murmuring to herself, and then she began scurrying about the kitchen, throwing various unidentifiable items into a blender.

"Don't be stingy girl, hand them over," she cackled, grabbing the basket from Ginny. She plopped three especially slimy lichen into the blender and pressed the button. "Prop his head up," she called, hobbling back over to Buttercup with the pitcher of blended goop, and before Libby could even ask what was going on, Sabine poured the stinky mixture down Buttercup's gullet.

"What are you doing?" gasped Libby.

"You want me to fix him, don't you?"

Libby wasn't sure how she should respond to that, but it didn't matter because in the next instant Sabine jabbed her finger toward the open door and commanded, "Liberty Frye, strange friend of Liberty Frye, take this goose out there!"

"My *name* is Ginny."

"And why are we supposed to take him outside?" added Libby.

"Because he's about to poop all over you," said Sabine, and they immediately scuttled out the front door, carrying Buttercup between them.

"What mess are you causing now?" demanded Wolfgang.

"Stay out of this, you Trottel!" Sabine snapped; the noise must have awoken Buttercup, who moaned loudly as Libby gently placed him on the ground.

"Schreckschraube!" Wolfgang bellowed back.

"Schwachkopf!"

"Schädling!"

"Drunk!" shrieked Sabine, her hands shaking violently at her sides, and at this, Wolfgang drew himself up, his purple face bulging in outrage so that even Sabine cowered just a little, and he breathed in and out very loudly for at least ten seconds.

"Dhat may be so," he finally replied, his voice straining under the effort to control his temper. "But it has nodhing to do widh dhe fact dhat you have just risked her life," and he pointed to the open doorway where Libby bent fretfully over Buttercup, "all for somedhing you know very well has *nodhing* to do widh getting Gretchen and Peter back."

"I don't have time for this," snapped Sabine, turning her horrid face toward the door. "What's the status on that goose?"

"He's ... going, I think," called Libby.

"You sent her after her backpack because of dhe book! You've wanted it for years! Isn't it why you betrayed Gretchen in dhe first place?"

"Ewww," squealed Ginny.

"I did no such thing!" huffed Sabine. "It isn't *my* fault that Klaus came to me for help all those years ago."

"Firlefanz!" yelled Wolfgang. "It's time you told us dhe truth before dhis gets any worse dhan it already is!"

"I don't involve myself with family matters!" Sabine yelled back, to which Wolfgang looked like he might actually choke on his rage.

"What do you dhink all of dhis stems from, woman?" he roared, but before Sabine had a chance to respond, he answered for her: "From *you* involving yourself in family matters!"

"Which is why I don't involve myself in them!"

And then Sabine grabbed a wooden spoon, stomped out the front door and poked it at Ginny. "Sort through it with this," she snapped. "Look for the undigested ones."

Ginny opened her mouth to protest, but she took one look at Sabine's dreadful expression and thought better of it. Slowly, she took the spoon, pressed her lips tightly together, held her nose and began digging around with her free hand, but not before she threw a dirty look Libby's way.

Libby glanced miserably from Ginny to Sabine and then back to Buttercup, who was whimpering and looking extremely bewildered by what had just happened, and she fought the urge to run screaming into the woods. Everything was going exactly opposite as planned, and worse, she knew that it was all her fault, especially for involving Wolfgang, who seemed more bent on giving Sabine a piece of his mind than on rescuing her parents, not to mention poor Buttercup.

"Tell us dhe trudh!" bellowed Wolfgang from the kitchen. Sabine spun around to face him.

"Fine! You want the truth? I'll tell it to you, but don't let me hear you say I didn't warn you!"

"Please stop yelling at each other, we're not going to get anywhere at this rate!" pleaded Libby, feeling rather desperate, because even with her limited experience in these matters, it seemed fairly evident that an argument between an enraged German baker and a disgruntled witch could never end well— but just then, a partially digested berry zipped through the air and bounced off her cheek.

"Sorry—slipped," gulped Ginny.

"Where is it?" cried Sabine, grabbing a pair of tongs and hobbling back outside; Ginny glanced at Libby, gesturing with her spoon.

"You've ... got a little brown spot, just there ...."

Sabine plucked the slimy piece of berry from the ground, inspecting it closely. "Not a great sample," she frowned. "I'll need at least two more, and try to make them less eaten, girl, will you?"

And with that, she marched inside with her tong of berry.

❀

CHAPTER 17

When Libby reached the kitchen sink, Sabine was slinging pots and pans around, all the while throwing some very nasty looks in Wolfgang's general direction.

"You were about to explain what happened," he reminded her, and although he had to speak loudly over all the clatter, at least he wasn't yelling anymore.

Sabine sniffed in response, taking a moment to collect her thoughts. Libby turned on the sink faucet and scrubbed her face with something in a squeeze bottle that she ardently hoped was soap.

"When Gretchen began learning the ways of Hexenkunst, it triggered something neither of us expected," Sabine replied huffily. "How was I supposed to have known? Before Gretchen, I'd never been a part of the Coven of Hessen; I didn't understand the ties. It was not until Zelna showed up at my house that I realized."

"Realized what?" growled Wolfgang.

Sabine sighed, waving her tong in the air impatiently. "That her studies were linking into a shared consciousness, obviously!"

Libby froze mid-rinse and glimpsed questioningly up at Wolfgang, but he looked just as confused.

"What's dhat supposed to mean?"

"It means that the Coven of Hessen is tied into itself, a form of synchronicity, if you will," explained Sabine, who refused to look at Wolfgang now, so she stared straight at Libby. "The more your mother learned, the more Zelna became aware of her learning and in turn, threatened by it.

THE FRUIT OF BARVULTMIR

It was impossible to foresee, of course, but I can't think of another reason why she knew so much about your mother. After all, Giselle hadn't spoken to her sister in years, much less introduce her to Gretchen!"

Wolfgang thought this over. "How do you explain dheir wedding day dhen?" he eventually asked. "I know you met widh Zelna dhat day!"

Sabine nodded in response as she plucked various ingredients from a cupboard, and none of them, thought Libby, looked like anything that remotely belonged in a kitchen. "Fetch me the toenail shavings, will you? The medium-sized one," she barked, and to Libby's dismay, she knew exactly what Sabine was looking for.

She went over to the fireplace and picked up the beaker, where it had been left by the vegetable chair, and returned to the kitchen with a shudder, sincerely hoping that this would be the only time in her life when toenails were actually considered an ingredient. She watched as Sabine grabbed the beaker, unplugged the rubber stopper and gave it a good sniff.

"Ripe!" she declared with satisfaction. "Just the right hint of toe!" and then she sprinkled a good three tablespoon's worth into a stone bowl, looking inordinately pleased at the process.

"The baker is correct," she continued peevishly. "Zelna did visit me, but it is not what he assumes. As I mentioned, Zelna became increasingly aware of your mother as Gretchen grew deeper into her studies, and she learned of Gretchen's plans to wed—but it wasn't because of anything *I* ever said," she paused, pursing her lips as she considered the bowl of toenails, and then she thrust it at Libby and pointed to a pestle. "Grind these up," she commanded. "I want them powdery; no edges to choke on, mind you!"

Libby blanched at the directive, but she glanced out the door where Ginny was still digging around with a spoon and decided she'd better not complain. She took the bowl of toenails and began to pummel them, trying her best to pretend that the crunchy sound was only coriander seeds, just like her mother taught her to do when they cooked chicken masala,

"Zelna saw something in their union that she wanted to stop," resumed Sabine, "and she must have approached Giselle for her help in preventing the wedding, knowing that Giselle would never want to be parted from her daughter, and knowing, too, that there was something your grandmother wanted, beyond anything else …."

"Klaus' fortune," harrumphed Wolfgang. "Dhat's why she married him in dhe first place, isn't it?"

"You should know," snickered Sabine, and Wolfgang's face, which had slowly returned to normal, flushed pink again. Sabine lifted a bald eyebrow. "In any case, Giselle never understood what she was getting herself into. She never does, it seems."

"I've got three, and that's all I'm doing," Ginny announced from outside.

"Don't get cheeky!" snapped Sabine, shuffling once more through the door and plucking the slimy berries from the ground. Buttercup wobbled away as fast as he could from her, settling a safe distance off, and Libby noticed with relief that everything except the tips of his tail feathers had returned to white. "For the sake of Kreitenzeilger, girl," she barked as she plunked the berries into a strainer, "get inside and wash yourself! You stink."

Ginny glared at everyone, but stomped into the house all the same, marching straight to the sink where she began to scrub her hands. Sabine shuffled in after her.

"It's the one family matter I did meddle in, to my great detriment—well aside from teaching Gretchen, but that was different—it was her birthright. I suppose you'll need to know, anyhow, and since it concerns me, well, I don't see why I shouldn't tell you," she paused to place the strainer of berries under the faucet, nudging Ginny away in the process, and as she watched the water rinse over them, her expression grew far away, as if events from long ago played out before her eyes. Libby held her breath and waited.

"Giselle was very beautiful, you see. It was an asset that came in handy in our younger years, especially when Klaus—your grandfather—came along. He had recently moved to Hanau to conduct research on the Fairy Tale Road; he was so quiet and ... refined, like someone who had been protected from the coarseness of everyday life." She smiled wistfully, still looking into the sink where the water swirled over the strainer.

"At the time, I worked at the Hanau Rathaus as a sort of cultural expert on all things Brothers Grimm related—that was *my* double life." She winked at Libby. "It was in Hanau that they were born, you see, and Klaus was determined to start his journey at their birthplace. And so for several weeks, we would meet at their statue in the marketplace, and we would speak of the Brothers Grimm and of the stories they collected throughout the land, which would become the modern fairy tales—like *Snow White* or *Red Riding Hood* or *Cinderella*—that you know today. Klaus' family was a great patron of their preserved work. His great-grandfather had translated many of the original tales into English years and years before and had a limited number of bound copies made. Klaus even had one in his possession. He'd shown it to me once. It was beautiful, of hunter green leather, and it contained such stories as I've never seen re-iterated elsewhere, not even at our museum."

Libby paused mid-toenail. "I know it!" she exclaimed. "That's the one I brought!"

Sabine blinked back at her as if she'd forgotten Libby was there.

"Oh, well, yes! Of course you did," she replied, straightening her posture. She shook the strainer for a moment and then carried it back to the counter. "Giselle knows the key to the fortune is hidden there, you see, but it isn't a secret *she* can get to," Sabine added with a chuckle, and then her expression instantly soured; she pressed her lips together and glared moodily at nothing in particular. "But I was speaking of Klaus," she resumed, lighting a candle. She carefully transferred the berries into a large test tube, filled it halfway with water, and began swirling it over the flame.

"Klaus told me that he was writing a book on a journey he

would take, traveling by foot to each town along the Fairy Tale Road—the same path in life that Jacob and Wilhelm Grimm took—starting from their birthplace in Hanau to the final destination in Bremen, recording facts along the way regarding the folktales that they had gathered. He was so very serious," she nodded fondly, "and he was convinced from all of his studies that the stories—the original ones, mind you, not the fairy tale versions that you see in cartoon movies today—were *real*, based on actual things that actually happened. Well, naturally, I was inclined to agree and told him of my own … studies. I thought he would be shocked; after all, our modern society does not understand things such as the craft I have devoted my life to, but he wasn't. He was perfectly willing to accept the idea that witches were still alive today—even pleased, as if I were living proof that his theory on the Grimms' tales was true …." Sabine trailed off, her expression once again filled with great sadness.

"Even *bad* witches?" Libby asked, and her voice came out in a whisper. "He was glad of that, too, of even people like Zelna?"

"Your grandfather was rather naïve in a way," sighed Sabine, "and he practically inhabited the world of those stories. It was his passion; I don't think it ever occurred to him that he could become a victim of the thing he had devoted his life to. But that's how it is for all of us, isn't it? Somewhere along the line, our greatest passions also become our deepest sorrows."

From the far corner of the room, a clock chimed two

times, instantly bringing Libby back to the present. "So what happened?" she prompted.

Sabine's head and shoulders heaved, as if recalling something she'd rather forget.

"Three days after Klaus set off for the town of Alsfeld, another stop on the Fairy Tale Road after Hanau, he abruptly returned, and quite to my surprise, announced to me that he and Giselle were engaged," she answered flatly. "Well, to say the least, I was shocked; I had no idea that Klaus and Giselle even knew each other! But what was I to do? Anything other than congratulations would have been … inappropriate." She paused and glanced over at Libby, a sad, bitter smile flicking over her face. "Merely a month after he made this announcement, they were married." Sabine shrugged. "And that was the end of our happy friendship. I only saw Klaus once more after that time."

"I'm surprised you actually had a friend to start with," muttered Ginny under her breath, and Wolfgang snickered in agreement.

"But why?" Libby asked, throwing a scowl their way.

Sabine stared wanly into the flame. "I wondered the same, but I had my suspicions. However, about a year after your mother was born, Klaus came to see me. He was a terrible sight; I nearly didn't recognize him—and I certainly wasn't prepared for what he asked me to do. I did my best, of course, but, well, that brings us here, doesn't it?" she looked up at Libby, her expression suddenly mocking. "Obviously, my best was … lacking."

"What did he ask you to do?" Libby asked, and Sabine

immediately turned her attention back to the test tube, her mouth twisting with some unspoken agitation. Libby stood very still, not daring to speak or move for fear of upsetting her, and her mind raced more than ever with questions.

"Klaus had brought with him his book—the heirloom of original fairy tales," Sabine replied. "He asked that I create a rune over it, so that what he was about to write within would not be visible to anyone except the person intended. And then, he asked for something to forget what he'd done, so that even he would not be able to betray his secret."

"Did you do it?" growled Wolfgang.

"Oh yes," chuckled Sabine, but her laugh was brittle. "I did just what he asked: I created a rune and gave him a potion made from the fruit of Barvultmir. Klaus returned home and I never saw him again. Life went on as usual. Years went by and then, one day, Gretchen and I met. *She* had actually sought *me* out, hearing that I had some link to her family's past. We began to form a friendship," she paused, pursing her lips as she inclined her head toward Wolfgang. "He hated that, of course—I think it was jealousy, although Gretchen never told me, because all she ever wanted was for the two of us to get along. Oil and water, I'd tell her."

"More like oil and vinegar," grumbled Wolfgang, but Sabine just rolled her eyes in response.

"She was already a young woman by the time I started to teach her the healing arts of Hexenkunst, and only about one year after that, well, I had the visit." She grimaced and, grabbing Libby's bowl of ground toenails, pinched up some of the powder and dropped it into the test tube, swirling it around once more, and with each swirl, Sabine grew more and more agitated. "It was the day of your parents' elopement, in fact, when Zelna came to see me," she resumed bitterly, "accusing me of conspiring with Klaus to hide something from her sister. Well, I denied it, of course, but to no avail. The visit escalated into a heated argument—all sorts of things long buried between us were brought up—and when it became clear that I would not cooperate, Zelna threatened me with what she knew I held most dear …." Sabine stopped and closed her eyes.

"What was that?" whispered Libby.

"Barvultmir, of course," she replied, and her voice came out in a moan. "His fruit created the essence for nearly all of my powers, and there was only one of him, for only one can ever be. I was terrified of losing him, and so I … I betrayed your grandfather, and in a way, betrayed Gretchen, but it isn't the way *he* thinks," she spat, glaring again at Wolfgang.

Ginny, who had been trying to stay as far away from Sabine as possible, suddenly stepped forward, her eyes wide with interest. "But what did you do?"

Sabine raised a limp hand and let it drop.

"I disclosed that, only through Klaus' bloodline, would the secret in his book be revealed. Zelna destroyed Barvultmir anyway, cursing his seed so that it could never grow from my hands. It was her insurance, I suppose, a way to make sure I never meddled in her business again, for without Barvultmir, I am nothing but an old hag who speaks to trees and stars. Maybe a few medicinal remedies, but nothing more," she shrugged, glancing up at Libby, a slow, scornful smile flitting across her withered lips. "And *that*, Liberty Frye, is what happens when you meddle in family affairs."

Wolfgang muttered something under his breath, but Libby was too busy trying to piece it all together to pay him any attention. It was a lot to digest, and there was still so much she didn't understand. "So, this … secret," she began, and the memory of that day in the attic came flooding back into her mind. "What my grandfather had written in his book has something to do with the treasure, doesn't it? That's what his will was saying, I think, something about his fortune."

"It would seem so," agreed Sabine. "Klaus never told me of his lineage; I suppose it wasn't something he wanted anyone to know—but somehow Zelna discovered the truth. She told me it was she who had informed her sister in the first place. It was the whole reason why Giselle had married him, thinking she would be rich for the rest of her life, not knowing Klaus had no intention of touching his inheritance. Of course, Zelna blamed me for getting in their way! Preposterous, but it doesn't matter now."

"So, that's what Grandmother wanted to prevent?" asked Libby, who was having a difficult time keeping up. "When my parents got married, is that what you were saying—that it's all about money?"

"There's far more to *that* story than I could begin to imagine," Sabine muttered. She turned away and stared sullenly at the test tube swirling between her fingers. The water was now black, and it looked thicker, too, with a strange smell that wafted under Libby's nose and made her suddenly think of licorice. Sabine must have noticed it as well, because she immediately lifted it away from the candle, tipping the tar-like contents into another beaker, and then she rapidly threw in an assortment of other ingredients from her bizarre inventory.

The liquid hissed as portions of ground armadillo tail and roasted brain coral flew into the mix, and the smell changed from licorice to something decidedly less pleasant. Libby wrinkled her nose, wondering how exactly this potion would be used to save her parents, and the thought reminded her of something else that had been nagging at her this whole time:

"All of this happened years and years ago, so why the wait? I mean, why is this all happening now?"

"Yes, I can see why you'd wonder that," Sabine grunted, reaching over to the container of sautéed octopus eye and spooning a generous portion into the beaker. "*Histoldvium Giessenvilden*," she whispered, swirling the beaker three times under her long, crooked nose, and Libby couldn't be sure, but it looked like one of Sabine's warts had actually lifted itself up and was now desperately wiggling away from her nostrils. "But, in fact, the timing couldn't be more perfect."

"You mean the Solstice of Arama?" guessed Libby, remembering their conversation from before, and Sabine nodded.

"Aramaar. And yes, that ... and something else," she said, grabbing a thin, metal spoon. She stirred the beaker until its contents grew thick. "That morning, after Zelna came to see me and destroyed Barvultmir, I knew something of vast importance must be at stake. She would never involve herself otherwise—I knew her well enough to know *that*. And so, I consulted everything at my disposal: books, charts, the trees, the stars … I worked feverishly all day, not resting for a moment, until I stumbled upon a clue."

"What?" breathed Libby.

"Your genealogy," she answered. "The Coven of Hessen, to be exact, which referred to two obscure stars I'd never paid attention to before. Well, between the lineage charts, the stars, and a bit of history from old Tufelwog—it's obnoxious what that elm won't tell you unless directly asked—I finally realized what you now already know: that with each step your mother took in her studies, the more Zelna could see of her. And I saw something else, too, something I knew your mother should be told as soon as possible, but I didn't have a chance until it was already too late.

"Your parents had left for Rothenberg, you see, and I had no way to reach them until afterwards, when everything had already happened. Well, that night, after Giselle tried to keep them from leaving, Gretchen came to see me with Peter, asking for help to heal his wound…. Naturally, she saw poor Barvultmir and guessed the rest, and it was then that I was finally able to tell her of my discovery. I did my best for your father, gave your mother the remaining seed I had managed to hide from Zelna, and then I told her to take Peter and flee from here, because what I had seen in the stars was something that made even my blood run cold."

"What did you see?" Ginny whispered.

"I saw what Zelna wanted to prevent," said Sabine,

"something of enormous potential, of a strength greater than any she could ever hope to possess."

"But what was it?" breathed Libby.

Sabine raised her grotesque face, her eyes burning straight into Libby's, and then in a low, still voice, she said:

"I saw *you*, Liberty Frye."

18

Passage to the Devil's Cave

"Himmelherrgott," murmured Wolfgang, but he might as well have been speaking to an empty room, because everyone else was too stunned to notice.

Even Sabine grew mesmerized by her own words, her expression far away, reliving the memories from that awful night, and Ginny gaped, dumbfounded, at Libby, and from the look on her face, it seemed as if she half expected her friend to have salamanders leaping out of her ears.

It was Libby who finally broke the silence.

"I thought ... I thought you couldn't see into the future," she blurted, and Sabine jerked her head up, as if she'd been shaken from a dream.

"What?"

"When you read the stars, you told me you could only see what was in the past, or some of the present," she began bewilderingly, and she wondered why, out of all things, *that* was the first thought to pop into her mind.

"Oh, yes, quite true," shrugged Sabine, her expression focusing back to her surroundings. "But I saw what Zelna saw, that's all. Believe me, it was enough to shake us all to the core! Gretchen and Peter left the next day," she paused, throwing a significant look at the baker, and his face was chalk-white. "I warned her to speak as little as possible to anyone—to blame me if she must for their departure."

"She didn't blame you," whispered Wolfgang, sinking onto a stool by the kitchen table. "Dhis whole time, I misunderstood what she was trying to tell me!"

Sabine took a sharp breath through her nose and then turned back to the dark, goopy substance in the beaker, carefully spooning it onto a strip of wax paper. Libby watched dazedly as the mixture cooled—her head swimming with a million questions—and it felt like her brain was just like that gloppy substance before her: formless and dark and containing things that were downright unnatural.

"Time for baking," announced Sabine, slipping the concoction into a covered cast iron pot and wobbling over to the fireplace. "Five minutes and eleven seconds, should do it. Nicely toasted, not too crispy." She furrowed her bald brows at some unspoken thought. She then resumed in a brusque voice, "But enough of the past, we've no time for that now. What is important is that you made it to the Cycle of Sicherheit, thank goodness, although admittedly in a less-than-ideal fashion. But I know one thing: without this orbit, you wouldn't stand a chance; there's no doubt about that!"

"This orbit?" repeated Libby, tearing her gaze from the pot that was making some very peculiar noises. "You mean ... like Mars or something?"

Sabine sniffed impatiently. "A rather dull comparison, Liberty Frye, binary solar systems are far more interesting! And before this cycle, you were on your first ellipse! That's always especially dangerous. Why, your mind was completely open—a blank page, so to speak!"

Libby thought that was a little unfair. After all, she might not make straight A's like Lamar Wilson, and she might not be pretty like Julie Lambert, and she definitely wasn't very popular, but one thing she did have going for her was an imaginative brain full of ideas.

Sabine must have understood.

"Oh, relax, child! I'm talking about your innocence, your lack of malice! It makes one decidedly indisposed to guarding against evil—pure, undiluted evil, mind you, which is clever and insidious—it can shape a mind before it even realizes it's been shaped; you wouldn't know what hit you! Someone like Zelna could easily take advantage of that, especially during one's first ellipse; she'd already gained access through your mother's portal, don't you know! If you had found out about her during that time, it would have been over for you, *Meluflen Kell Zutviell*, and that is that! She'd have seen you in an instant!"

"Oh," said Libby, feeling more than a little confused.

"So, you're saying dhat Libby has her own *star system*?" sputtered Wolfgang.

"Obviously, but that's hardly the point!" Sabine snapped, jabbing a crooked finger at Libby. "The point is, this girl has less than two hours left to reach the Devil's Cave and then ... well, if she'd done what I'd asked, she might stand a chance, but now, without the book, well I don't know, I just don't know!"

Libby wasn't sure how to best explain to Sabine why she'd come back empty-handed. In fact, she felt rather sheepish about leaving her bag in that window because it dawned on her that there may have been another reason altogether for it hanging there. She remembered the window being open ever so slightly, and she realized that it could have been there for Iorgu. After all, he had a knack for going through windows— maybe he was supposed to take it to Zelna, or even, straight to the Devil's Cave ....

Libby gulped nervously, because no one, not even a girl with her own solar system, relishes the prospect of disappointing a witch. Too late, she realized; Sabine was scowling as she flung herself into the vegetable chair by the fireplace.

"But I understand the significance of it now," she continued, chewing her bottom lip with a few wobbly teeth, and a faint lavender smell wafted from the chair, making Libby feel strangely sleepy. "Something I hadn't even foreseen myself!"

"Foreseen what?" managed Libby, trying not to yawn, and then she suddenly wasn't groggy anymore because Sabine turned her terrible stare on her, her pale eyes blazing with a fear Libby had never seen before, and it made her arm hairs prickle up like porcupine pins.

"Why, the rune, of course! It requires a few drops given willingly for Klaus' secret to be revealed," Sabine replied, twisting her hands in agitation. "I thought I was being clever at the time, protecting your mother from any forceful application, but now, well, don't you see? It's what Zelna is after!"

But Libby didn't see anything at all, except an ugly witch with a very unpredictable temper who kept speaking in riddles. Nervously, she shook her head.

"Kreitenzeilger, girl, it's obvious—you are part of the bloodline! *The key to the rune has passed to you!*" Sabine practically screeched, throwing up her hands, and Libby stared back at her, feeling her spine tingle as if an electric shock had gone right through it. The significance of the book sank in with a queasy feeling, and Libby looked despairingly from Sabine to the fire, knowing she couldn't have messed things up more if she had tried.

"Burning," she whispered.

"What?"

Libby pointed at the iron pot. "I ... think it's burning."

"Huch!"

Sabine grabbed a thick cloth by the chair and scuttled toward the pot, now lifting it gingerly from the fire.

"So is that why I'm here?" Libby managed to ask, doing her

best to ignore the churning in her stomach, "so that my blood can be used to reveal the secret?"

"If only you should be so lucky," grunted Sabine, shuffling over to the kitchen with the pot. Carefully, she placed it on the tabletop and stood there for a minute, gazing into the smoke curling from the lid. When she turned around once more, her face was filled with that same fear Libby had seen earlier. "But we must remember the Solstice of Aramaar. Zelna would never employ such extravagance for a mere *rune*, especially when the sum of all her powers—of the Coven of Hessen itself—is right there, within her grasp. No, Liberty Frye, if you do this, you are risking everything. You will have touched *evil*. Do you understand?"

Libby's spine radiated even more with tingles, washing goose-bumps over every inch of her, and her legs felt like jello. She leaned against the vegetable chair, wondering how she should respond, because the truth was she didn't understand at all. In fact, she had no idea what was going on or what to expect.

But that didn't matter, she realized. All that mattered was saving her parents.

She turned back to Sabine, clearing her throat to answer, but her esophagus felt like it had been tied into a knot, and she was feeling extremely woozy, the room drifting before her eyes like a shaken snow globe.

"Even if you do somehow manage to survive this, your world will never be the same," Sabine continued, as if sensing her resolution. "No more carefree childhood for you.

Live through this or die—either way you look at it, you'll be forfeiting your life."

"I have to find them," Libby whispered, and Sabine studied her for a long moment, inhaled sharply through her nose, and then dropped her fist on the table with a thud.

"Then I've nothing left to offer you but this," she said, lifting the top off the pot. She grabbed the baked potion in her gnarled hands, not even flinching from the heat, and broke it into three pieces with a quick twist of her wrists. She looked longingly at the blackened dust on her fingers. After a deep sigh, she turned to Libby once more. "The rest is up to you, because I dare not—no, I will not—face her again, not for anything in the world. So I'll ask you one more time, Libby: Are you *still* willing?"

Libby was in the process of responding when something dark zoomed through the doorway.

"Freddie, what's taken you so long? Stop that!"

Libby looked up to see a bat flapping excitedly over Sabine, squeaking in a manner that sounded almost as if he were trying to talk to her.

"You ... have a pet bat?"

"Don't you?" answered Sabine, raising her hand toward him, and from the other side of the room, Ginny jumped behind Wolfgang and promptly began chattering off rabies statistics, which did nothing to calm Freddie.

"What is it, Freddie? What's all the fuss? You two—be quiet! It's hard enough carrying a message, much less when you've got a speech impediment!"

The room fell silent. The bat settled down on a little swing Libby hadn't noticed before that hung from the kitchen rafters and proceeded to suck on a lemon. After a good minute, he delicately put the lemon down and squeaked again.

"What is it, yes, yes … no! Really! Oh, I don't believe it, you don't really say? Freddie, stuff and nonsense!"

Libby was pretty sure she saw the bat make a face, but in any case, he definitely made a huffy noise and then folded his wings in front of him, spinning around so that his back faced them all.

"What's he saying?" managed Libby, and Sabine tore her stunned expression from Freddie to look at her.

"He's saying … well, I can hardly believe it; I knew it was a long shot, I declare, I expected a begrudging yes, but I never dreamed …." She trailed off again, shaking her head in amazement.

Libby glanced from Sabine to Freddie, earnestly wishing she could speak bat.

"It is the honor of a century. Not even Guerginmuel standing in the way! I've never heard of such a thing before. Never! Especially not from the pines—they're always prickly—but Freddie says it, so it must be true," continued Sabine, to which Freddie slowly turned around on his swing and chirped something else. Sabine nodded. "He says there was a lengthy meeting on the matter, that's what took him so long, but in the end it was unanimous. Not the baker of course—he's far too fat, and besides, they don't trust him around the junipers."

"But what are you *talking* about?" sputtered Libby, and

Sabine sucked in her breath, blinking her bald eyelashes at nothing in particular. Freddie squeaked again, now flapping his wings this way and that as if trying to explain in pantomime, but that was hopeless, Libby discovered. Thankfully, Sabine calmed down enough to collect her thoughts.

"I'm saying you've got safe passage from Rodenbach all the way to Steinau, girl. Did you think you could just drive there? Certainly not—not so close to the gloaming—they'll be looking for you! But Freddie's solved that; he's found a steady line of evergreens: Silver Firs, Junipers, Blue Spruce, Scots Pine … they've all agreed to take you!"

The wind whipped Libby's cheeks and blew her hair so that it tangled now and then with the needles, but that was nothing compared to her stomach that leapt into her throat and down again every other second as she was catapulted from one tree to the next, zooming over the eaves of the evergreens. If it weren't for the old, raggedy coat Sabine had made her wear, she'd have been ripped to shreds from the sheer velocity of their movement. She couldn't quite believe it, but Ginny's random screams from behind her assured her that it wasn't a dream. She was just thankful that they were passing through a rather untraveled part of the woods.

The trees moved faster and faster, and soon, the entire forest was nothing but a blur; she no longer felt the scratches from their needles because she was moving so quickly that she barely made contact. The wind whistled in her ears and her eyes streamed from the cold—although it was also entirely possible that she was actually crying from the fright of it all.

An entire thirty minutes must have passed before things started to slow down. Libby noticed that the sky was beginning to dim just when an enormous fir passed her on to a smaller one with long, drooping needles and then, instead of traveling treetop to treetop, she dropped downwards, falling a foot or two each time before landing on the next row of springy branches. She knew better than to scream, but it was terrifying—much worse than flinging from tree to tree—and by the time she reached the ground, she had to sit for a minute or two before her legs stopped shaking.

When she finally looked around, she saw that she was sitting in a gravel parking lot. A sign depicting a cavern and adorned with the word "Teufelshöhle" loomed overhead with an arrow pointing to the left. Libby didn't have time to notice much else before Ginny landed with a thud beside her, and if it weren't for her purple and navy checkered coat, she could have passed for a ghost.

The wind instantly picked up, swirling dried leaves around the pair, and within the wind, a voice could be heard, moaning from the treetops; it seemed to be made up of hundreds, all rasping in unison, and after a while, Libby could just hear it say:

> *"The road is hard for those who search.*
> *The fields are full of living dead.*
> *And if you choose that narrow earth,*
> *Keep straight and look to where you tread.*

For if you don't, those visions bright,
Will lure you to the dreamers' grave.
No! Stay true, and look ahead,
For it is there you'll find the way."

The wind stopped swirling and something floated to the ground. It took a few seconds for Libby to realize what had just happened, but when she did, she reached out to pick up the object, thinking it must be some sort of note. And then, she drew back with a yelp because it suddenly glowed a pale yellow and fluttered into the air.

"It's ... a giant *firefly?*" gasped Ginny, but before they could really get a good look, it was already flitting between the two of them, clearly anxious to be followed. Libby and Ginny scrambled to their feet, and immediately, the object darted ahead.

19

THE SOLSTICE OF ARAMAAR

The ground sloped steeply as Libby and Ginny followed the pale glow.

The woods were completely silent, with only the crunch and slip of their steps filling the frosty air. To their left, the earth rose higher and higher above them, and to their right, mossy rocks and spindly, bare oaks created a tricky maze. There was no clear path to follow, only the dancing light of the firefly, and it didn't act at all concerned with the fact that they had to scramble over boulders and under logs to keep up.

It didn't help that the coat Libby had on was at least five sizes too large for her, and had a way of tangling up in her feet at the most inconvenient of times. She wished she would have remembered to change back into her own clothes before leaving Sabine's hut, but it was too late for that, so she tucked up the hem and did her best to keep up. Soon, they were passing a wide, cleared opening, complete with a wooden sign—obviously the main entrance to the Devil's Cave.

"Shouldn't we go through there?" puffed Ginny, pointing an unsteady finger at the cavern, but Libby shook her head, remembering the words of the evergreens, and gestured for them to continue.

It was now difficult to see; dusk settled into the forest, and if it were not for the glow of the firefly, Libby was sure they'd be lost. At one point, something white flashed in the distance, followed closely by a strange, mournful call, but when she glanced toward it, the firefly darted in front of her—practically smacking her right in the face—and then flew forward once more.

They pressed on, and even though Libby was determined to heed the warning of the trees, she couldn't help but wonder why they were being led along such a difficult route. They walked along a narrow, winding crevice that made it difficult not to trip, and just a little further to the right, there was nice, flat ground that headed in the same direction. She pushed forward regardless, but after stumbling over a rock and nearly twisting her ankle, she stepped aside for a moment, still following the firefly, but just not in its direct path. Ginny followed after her, not seeing the difference.

"What's that noise?" she whispered, and Libby frowned, hearing it, too; it was coming from the ground—whispery, scratching sounds. It was so distracting. She tried her best to ignore it, focusing on the firefly, but finally, she looked down.

Through the waning light, she saw something scuttle over her shoes. And then, she realized what it was: enormous spiders—black and hairy—and it took every ounce of her willpower not to scream. She bit her lip so hard she drew blood, but she brushed them off, and then she pushed Ginny back to their original pathway. Ginny lost her balance and stumbled forward, which was a good thing because it gave Libby just enough time to swat the three spiders crawling up Ginny's legs before she noticed.

"What are you doing?" Ginny hissed angrily.

"Sorry, tripped," gulped Libby, and she promptly followed the exact path of the firefly once more, never deviating a millimeter.

The moon was just drifting from the clouds, showing a sliver of its full glow, when they finally stopped. The firefly danced around a tall, shaggy tree with enormous roots that curled from the ground and stretched over portions of sunken earth like wide tendrils of vine, creating gaps just large enough to squeeze through. Libby stared from the firefly to the tree, hoping she had misunderstood.

"Does it think we're crazy?" gasped Ginny. "I'm not going in *there!*"

Libby shuddered in agreement, following Ginny's gaze

toward an especially treacherous looking gap in the ground, but the firefly zipped through it anyway and disappeared somewhere in the dark, earthy depths. Libby squeezed her eyes shut, trying very hard to forget about those spiders. "You can stay here, Ginny; it's probably safer—"

"Do you think I'm crazy?" said Ginny with a glare. "I'm not staying *here!*"

Libby would have laughed, but she was too terrified. She *hated* spiders; in fact, even her pet Oscar back home was part of a study in her science class; it was not for nothing that she chose him as the thing she feared the most …. She took another deep breath.

"Okay, well, here goes …." And then, before she could change her mind, she scrambled after the firefly, climbing over the twisted, woody roots and then slipping into the darkness. Ginny watched it all with a horrified expression, but in the next moment, Libby heard shuffling behind her followed by a muffled yelp. Seconds later, she could just see the whites of Ginny's eyes floating in the damp, still cavern.

"This is so spooky," trembled Ginny. "I can't believe we're actually doing this! There must be bats and snakes and-and creepy things."

"Worse," muttered Libby.

"Oh, look! There's our bug!"

Indeed, the yellow glow flitted before them, impatiently it seemed, and Libby and Ginny stumbled after it.

This time, Libby didn't dare look at the ground, even if she could have seen through the darkness, but it felt soft and springy, and at times it squished in a most disconcerting way, but her heart was pounding so hard that all she could do was concentrate on following the light ... and not hyperventilating.

They turned a rounded corner, and then two more, and Libby could see they were deep in the earth, the ground growing firmer beneath them, the walls cool and smooth, and as the glow of the firefly glanced off them, she could just see the pearlescent forms of stalactites dripping from the ceilings, oozing into eerie, animal-like shapes that looked almost purposefully formed. Another corner, and then—

Libby and Ginny found themselves inside a magnificent chamber; it was more like an underground cathedral, really, surrounded on all sides by statuesque stalactites and stalagmites, and the ceiling curved with perfect balance toward a circular opening in the middle.

The firefly looped in the air, flitting its wings as if in a wave, before darting towards the ceiling. It flew higher and higher through the vertical tunnel leading straight to the sky far above, until it disappeared altogether, leaving nothing for the cavern's illumination but the filtering moonlight that still battled with the clouds.

This was all very extraordinary, but even more so than that was what Libby saw directly in front of her. It was a thick, stone table, only two feet or so from the floor, and circling around it were etchings made within the ground, strange shapes that curled one into the other, and even though Libby could not begin to understand their meaning, it sent an ominous shudder down her spine.

She looked away.

Her eyes adjusted to the cavern's light, and as she gazed about her, something pale caught her eye in the shadows. Ginny saw it, too.

"*Mummies!*" she choked.

And it did look that way at first, because beyond the stone table, two pale, tall forms could just barely be seen; their faces glowed strangely in the darkness, and they were each covered with a white blanket and laid upon a slanted portion of the cave, so that their bodies reclined at an angle. Even in their ghostly pallor, Libby would have recognized them anywhere.

"Mom and Dad!"

She ran toward them with her heart in her throat, fumbling into Sabine's coat pockets at the same time, and her hands caught on all sorts of things but the one thing she wanted. Out plopped a lizard and then two sticky, partially used chapsticks. A wad of grey hair. Three-quarters of an apricot and a ribbiting, one-legged frog.

Finally, she gripped the velvety satchel holding all the hope she had left in the world.

"*S achen Tuweil Fefea,*" she gasped, reciting the first line from memory—she'd repeated it over and over again in her head during the voyage over the treetops. She glanced down at her left hand to read the notes scribbled across the palm.

"*Viehelden Mir Tulcea,*" she continued, now opening the satchel, but her fingers felt like they'd been dipped in oil, because everything kept slipping from her grip. She strained up on her toes, and she could just reach her mother's face, but her hands were shaking so much that it was hard to read the spell, balance the bag, and grab the dried section of potion at the same time, not to mention the fact that already, she could feel the effects of uttering those words. She fell back on her heels, frustrated, peering into the shadows for something to use.

"Let me help," Ginny was saying, taking the satchel. Carefully she pulled out a piece of the charcoal-like substance. "Just tell me when you're ready …."

Libby nodded in appreciation, not daring to break the spell she had already begun. *"Meluflen Kell Zutviell,"* she said, taking the piece from Ginny's hands, and then up she went, standing on her toes; she was face-to-face with her mother, who was as pale and as still as death. *"Tusichen Lail Matqiel!"* she shouted, opening her mother's mouth and pushing the charcoal between her teeth.

She fell back, feeling weak in the knees from the exertion, but there was no time to rest. She turned to her father, and she was concentrating so hard she didn't feel the sweat pouring off her, drenching her clothes and even her coat. Ginny placed the second portion in her hand, and then Libby was standing on tiptoes once more, leaning over her father as she pried open his mouth.

> *"Sachen Tuweil Fefea,*
> *Viehelden Mir Tulcea,*
> *Meluflen Kell Zutviell,*
> *Tusichen Lail Matqiel!"*

She shoved the potion into his mouth and then collapsed against the cavern wall, and not a minute too soon. She was absolutely exhausted. And amazed. Sabine had warned her that it would take all of her strength, but she had no idea just how draining a spell could be! Her arms and legs felt watery, and her eyes were heavy, so heavy, and her brain felt like a bowl of buttered grits; even thinking was difficult.

Feebly, she motioned toward the satchel in Ginny's hands. "I'm ready for mine," she managed, anxious to regain her strength, but Ginny was shaking her head, her face pale and frightened.

"I saw the way she was looking at it," she whispered. "I didn't think she would—"

"Please … the other piece," panted Libby.

"But Sabine m-must have *taken* it!" Ginny wailed, now shaking the bag upside down.

Libby stared back at her, not understanding what she was saying, but Ginny's mouth was still moving even though the words sounded muddled and far away. Libby felt her back against the cool wall, slowly slipping to the ground, and she was tired, so tired … and what was Ginny saying because it sounded more like a shriek, no, but that wasn't Ginny at all, was it?

"That vas a dirty trick," murmured a voice, and Libby fought to open her eyes.

This was difficult to do; in fact, everything about her felt heavy. She tried to focus on her hands. They were resting on something smooth, palms down. She was lying on something, she determined, something hard but cool to the touch. She could feel the presence of someone near her, too, because even in the damp air, warmth radiated just above her right shoulder.

She concentrated on her eyes once again. They began to open, slow and heavy, as if weights were somehow tied to her lashes, another lift, and then—

The blast of silvery moonlight spilled over her. It was all that she could see, pulsing in from far above, channeling directly to where she lay. *So I am on the stone table*, she realized.

A muffled shout came from somewhere beyond, and when she could finally coordinate with her brain to turn her head, her eyes flung wide open with fear. Zelna stood over her, eagerly watching her every move. Iorgu lurked just behind, and it took a moment for Libby to realize he was holding Ginny back, moving her away from the table.

"Just in time, Liberty Frye," murmured Zelna, smoothing away strands of hair from Libby's face, and her touch was tender, like a mother's, and it made Libby's skin crawl.

She struggled to move away, but she couldn't, her legs and arms were still too heavy; even her voice felt bogged down somehow. How long had she been unconscious? She tried to clear her throat, desperate to regain control of herself; she knew that the first thing she had to do was to somehow get Ginny out of the cave ....

"This isn't her fault," Libby managed to croak, her throat aching from the effort. "If you let her go, I'll do whatever you want!"

This was met with a low, amused chuckle.

"But you already have," replied Zelna, leaning over her so that Libby stared straight into those jewel-green eyes. "You've done exactly as I've vanted, all along!"

Libby blinked, her mind racing in confusion; she wanted to look away so that she could think straight, but try as she might, she couldn't tear her gaze away from those eyes.

"You didn't think I intended to rouse your parents, did you? I need all of *my* energy for vhat lies ahead," smiled Zelna. It was unnerving, the way she was smiling—it was genuinely warm, adoring even, and it was more terrifying than any glare in the world.

"You … *wanted* me to wake them?" she whispered, and Zelna nodded slowly.

"You'll understand soon enough. These things cannot be rushed—it is a lesson you've never learned, I think, to vait. It takes patience, years and years of careful planning, but then this!" she raised her arms to the moonlight, her face alive with triumph. "It is glorious, a beautifully timed puzzle! Even Sabine's piece fell in perfectly!"

Libby rolled her head away with a groan. She needed a moment to think; it seemed impossible what Zelna was saying, impossible that she had *wanted* Libby to come here all along, impossible that Sabine was somehow part of the plan, but that was what Zelna was saying, wasn't it?

She stared up at the cavern's ceiling, remembering now the last thing before she'd lost consciousness:

The third piece, she recalled, seeing Ginny's white, terrified face. Sabine had kept the third piece, the last part of the potion that she was supposed to take to regain her strength.

But why?

And already, she knew the answer. Ginny had said it: the way Sabine had looked at that potion with such longing—the last remnant from the Tree of Fire—as if to hand the thing over was to hand over her heart and soul. . . .

"Sabine would never help you," Libby said, but she wished she could feel that certain.

"Oh, there are different vays of helping," replied Zelna, entirely unconcerned. "It is like a chess game: you have to know your opponent, anticipate their every move and reaction, make them believe their choices are their own and not vhat you have set them up to be. The trick is, to find out their price," she confided. "You find the price, you know the person. Everyone has a price."

"I don't have a price," whispered Libby, but Zelna lifted her brows mockingly.

"Of course you do. It is different for everyone, but it is alvays something valued above all else."

Libby swallowed, trying to calm the thumping in her chest. Zelna smiled tenderly.

"For *you*, my sweet, it is your goodness. And goodness vill always be used against you. If you vould just be a little less loyal, a little less brave and determined to save your family . . . if you vould have just dissolved into tears and vorried more about yourself, accepting your fate like most people—and ve are all of us sincerely glad that you did not—vell, you vouldn't be here now, vould you?" and before Libby could digest that thought, Zelna continued, her voice echoing in the cavern.

"For Emil, it vas his conscience, but because he vas too veak to truly account for his choices, he vent on instinct, and in so doing, led you right into my plan," she sighed, shaking her head. "I'm sure he has already met vith his just desserts, poor fool. But for Sabine, the price vas shamefully low: just a vhiff of that power she once took for granted. It is like a drug to her, a taste is all that's needed."

"Sabine was helping us," glared Libby, unwilling to believe Zelna's awful words. "She risked everything to do it!"

"She *meant* to help you," nodded Zelna, looking far too pleased by Libby's reaction. "She alvays *means* to help, but in the end, vell … it goes back to vhat I was saying. Ve all have a price."

"And what's yours?" Libby demanded angrily, to which Zelna's face grew serious once more. Her stillness was like a vacuum, sucking in everything around, and she continued to look down at Libby with such an intense, hungry focus that for a few seconds, Libby forgot to breathe.

"My price is the rarest thing of all," she eventually whispered.

The hairs on the back of Libby's neck instantly bristled into pins; she had no idea what Zelna meant, but she didn't dare ask. She was beginning to panic. Everything was upside down.

She had been used, she knew that much, used in the worst way, because she'd somehow betrayed her own family and worse, dragged Ginny along for the ride. She could feel sweat forming at her temples, and her breath was becoming quick and shallow. She had to think about something else, she had to calm down. So she said the first thing that came to mind: "Where's Grandmother?"

"Your grandmother!" laughed Zelna, genuinely surprised. "You didn't think she'd be *here*, did you?"

"But I thought she wanted the rune—the key to the book," Libby blurted, trying to sound strong, but the truth of it was that she had never felt more helpless and scared in her entire life. She forced herself to look away from Zelna, now searching the shadows of the cavern in an attempt to spot Ginny, but the moonlight made it impossible for her to see anything beyond the direct glow around her. "Ginny," she called desperately. "Are you okay?"

"Hhmm!"

"Your friend is fine," Iorgu's voice floated from the darkness. "Just a little speechless at the moment."

"And don't vorry about your grandmother," smiled Zelna. "Giselle vill get the rune alright, straight from you. In fact, she is probably sitting up as ve speak, just vaiting for that knock on the door! It's the least ve can do for her cooperation."

"She's *expecting* me?"

"I promised no harm vould come to you or your mother. That vas *her* price, you know—that and the rune," Zelna was saying, indifferent to Libby's shock. "But it is all a distraction, a prop to use against her for control, and it vorked. She's grown obsessed vith the idea, like a fly beating against a vindow vhen the door stands vide open. She's blinded, convinced she needs my help, vhen all along, the solution vas in her grasp."

Libby didn't know what to make of that, nothing made sense, because it sounded to her as if Zelna was not the least bit interested in the treasure....

"But the thing I did not anticipate vas our visitor," continued Zelna, rolling her eyes in the general direction of Ginny. "And your pet goose! Meine Güte! Now, that vas a delightful surprise! Vhy, I had that bag hanging there, just vaiting for you for hours! But I enjoyed puzzling that piece, indeed, yes, I did. Remarkable! And vhile I am not so taken by your human acquaintance, I am glad she came; it solves a dilemma I vas having. It is so difficult to know in these circumstances; indeed, impossible: How do you know if vhat you remember is *authentic*? If vhat you feel is *genuine*? But now, vith her help, I vill see," she paused for a moment to look up at the moonlight filling the cavern. "Iorgu, bring her here!"

Libby heard shuffling and some struggle, but in the next moment, Ginny's terrified, tear-streaked face loomed beside her. A strip of material was tied around her mouth and she was holding Libby's backpack in her arms.

"This is your best friend, is it not?" Zelna asked in a low voice.

"The best friend anyone could ever have."

"She vould do anything for you, vouldn't she?"

"I hope not," whispered Libby, and her throat felt like it

was tearing. "Ginny, don't listen to her; whatever it is, don't do what she says!"

"But all I vant is for her to give you your bag!" replied Zelna, and Ginny jumped forward a little, as if she'd been prodded, shakily lifting the backpack onto the table where Libby lay. Libby felt the canvas next to her arm, and then she felt her hand being lifted so that it rested on top of it. "My goodness, you do suspect the vorst in everything! It's just your bag, after all! A simple test. Vhen the time comes, ve vill see if I—I mean you—vill remember."

Libby thought about this for a moment, trying to make heads or tails of it, but it was no use. She glanced up at the light again, and she saw that the moon was almost dead center now; she knew she had to stall for time until she could at least move. Without her strength, they didn't stand a chance....

"What about my parents?" she asked, and she saw that Ginny was still standing there and from the look on her face, Libby knew that she was trying to tell her something. She glanced back at her helplessly, not understanding, but she noticed that Ginny was working her mouth under the gag, as if to get around it. "What will you do with them?"

"*Do* vith them?" repeated Zelna. "Vhy, nothing—you've already done the vork for me! By the time they are fully awake, they'll not know a thing that has happened. They'll see you, see your grandmother, and vonder vhy they've lost a whole veek of time. A strange illness, you'll say, you've been so vorried, you'll cry with relief, and they'll believe you. You'll all go home none the viser and then, vhen the time is right, you, Liberty Frye, vill mysteriously disappear. That vill be the true tragedy for your parents. But they'll have had time before then to vonder vhat has happened to their sveet daughter they once loved; indeed, by the time you leave, they might even be relieved!"

"They'd never do that—and I'd never leave them," said Libby, but her head was racing. Whatever it was that Zelna had planned, it must be something awful, something that would change who she was so that she was no longer herself—a monster, even. And then, it occurred to her that her fingers were nervously picking at the patches on her bag; she must be regaining her strength, she realized. She glanced back at Ginny, who was making strange faces in the same direction.

"Remember your left pocket—" Ginny gasped out, working her upper lip over the cloth, but then Iorgu lunged at her and her voice grew muffled once more as she disappeared into the shadows.

Libby stared after her, but all she could see was darkness beyond. "So ... about my parents," she improvised, stalling for time. "What was *their* price?"

Zelna looked bored.

"It is like that Russian author said," she shrugged, and then she bent down as if to find something that was stored under the table. "Some dribble about happy families are all the same, but unhappy families are each unhappy in their own vay?"

Something crunched below her; Libby struggled to look, but even straining every muscle, she could only manage to swivel onto her side. Well, at least it was progress. "What—

what's that supposed to mean?" she pressed, trying to keep the conversation going.

"It means you and your parents are predictable," replied Zelna, poking her head above the table once more. "Goodness and happiness come from the same source, do they not? Love, loyalty, innocence—and all the blindness that goes vith it. All it took vas one exquisitely charmed, manipulating letter to enhance those feelings. That took care of your mother; she's been torn vith guilt about vhat happened all those years ago when she eloped, convinced if she had done things differently, she might have been able to part on better terms, to at least say goodbye to her father. Nonsense, of course, but that is vhat your grandmother had her believe. Giselle blamed vhat happened on her nerves—on the medication she'd been switched to that sent her into a moment of rage, desperate to keep your mother from leaving at all costs, even to the point of stabbing Peter! And Gretchen believed it, not knowing the *real* reason vhy Giselle didn't want her to go.

"Your father vas even easier; tragic, really, that I invested so much time pondering him. He just vants her to be happy! How such a man can betray his own judgment vill never cease to disgust me. Vell, long story short, they just folded, helpless as babes, the both of them. The hard part vas the finding," smiled Zelna, and her eyes sparked with something that made Libby temporarily forget about everything but those terrifyingly alert, jewel-green eyes. "Your mother hid you vell, Liberty Frye."

Libby forced herself to look away. There was something magnetic about Zelna's stare, something horribly wrong with it, as if each time she looked into her eyes, she felt almost as if she were not just looking, but *going into* them.

"So … if all you want is me, why didn't you just take me? Why go to all of this trouble?" grasped Libby desperately. She could sense Zelna's impatience, and beyond that, she was running out of things to say, not to mention those eyes, every time she looked at them.…

But Zelna was smiling down at her, that same adoring smile, and Libby heard a loud gulp come from somewhere in her throat, and she had to look away.

"Because, my dear, it is just like that rune of yours," Zelna replied sweetly, nodding toward the backpack resting under her arm. "Or, for that matter, anything vorth having. You can cheat a little, manipulate the circumstances, but you can never force it. You have to vait for things to come to you on their own."

And it was as if the stars had been waiting for those words to come to *them*, because the light blazed brighter, and Libby looked up to see the moon directly above, spilling over her and the stone table where she lay, filling the entire cavern with its glow.

20

Changeling

She could see Ginny now, standing beside Iorgu, who had momentarily forgotten his grasp on her. The moon gushed over them all, and Zelna's face paled, her eyes blazing with excitement.

"The time has come," she announced, now walking in a circle around the stone table where Libby lay. "You asked me vhat my price vas. Vell, I vill tell you: my price is you, Liberty Frye. You, who are everything I've always yearned to be—vhat you could do! And yet you squander it, living out a rather unremarkable life with two of the most overprotective parents I have ever vitnessed! They smother you! They deny your greatness! It is the most horrendous crime of all—the greatest betrayal. But I have come to fix that," she murmured, tracing her hand along Libby's face, and it was a terrible thing to lay there, feeling that cold, dry touch. Unconsciously, Libby started, her fingers fidgeting at the canvas of her bag, strong enough to grip ….

"Sabine has told you of your significance, has she not?" Zelna purred, and Libby froze, not daring to look away.

"She told me that I am a witch …."

"Not just a witch!" cried Zelna. "You are the last of our coven, of the Witches of Hessen! Each of our generation grows stronger than the last—do you know vhat this makes you?"

And Libby shook her head, not knowing how she should respond or what she should do.

"It makes you capable of things I have only dreamed of … until now!"

Libby realized she was still gaping back at Zelna, transfixed by those bright eyes, and she felt that same strange tug, as if she were somehow slipping into Zelna's stare. Or maybe, she began to wonder, maybe it was the other way around, as if those piercing eyes were somehow sinking into *her*. Libby gulped and tore her gaze away, concentrating on the feel of the canvas bag below her fingers, now squeezing it nervously. Something inside met her grasp.

"It's all there!" came Ginny's voice, and Libby turned her head to seek her in the blazing moonlight. Ginny was only about twenty feet away; Iorgu held her by the arms once again, but she had managed to slip off her gag somehow, and she was nodding furiously at Libby, her huge, brown eyes practically springing from their sockets, bulging in the direction of the bag.

And then, Libby remembered. Of course. Why hadn't she thought of it before?

"At first—when I first learned of your existence, I vanted to destroy you," Zelna continued, her expression still eager, but she seemed to grow distracted by whatever thought it was that germinated in her mind. "The threat of your power vas too great. It should not have been difficult—all it vould take vas the right move at the right time, my spell vould have done the rest. But vhen your grandmother failed all those years ago, I thought she had ruined everything. It took me years to see vhat potential I had almost vanquished! True, there have been sacrifices along the vay, and the blood of youths spilled to keep me strong enough for this very hour, but it is all vell vorth it now. Through the Star of Aramaar, I vill never need that again, for I vill have all the power and knowledge to unleash vhat you leave dormant!"

Libby's hand fumbled about in her bag. She had managed to get to the left pocket, and now, it was just a matter of coordinating things.

"What do you want from me?" she said, or at least, she *thought* she had ....

"Do you not feel it?" replied a quiet voice.

Libby gasped, staring back at Zelna, and the glow of moonlight pulsed all around her, rippling in waves like an electric current, pulling and tugging at her mind. She fought it, knowing she had one chance left before it was too late, and knowing, too, that however incredible it seemed, Zelna was not going to kill her. No, it was something far worse.

The light bounced and twisted between them, and Libby struggled not to look, she felt pulled into it, just like that feeling of Zelna's eyes. Already, she felt the push, her head spinning with fantastic images, of power, of freedom, of all the things in the world she could do and have and see and she wouldn't be stuck in that stupid school where everyone made fun of her, or at home where her parents always kept secrets, she wouldn't be treated like a silly child, no, no, never again, and she could do anything and go wherever she wanted ....

"We'll have youth, a new life to begin again—anything our heart desires!" cried Zelna, her voice echoing in the cavern, but no, Libby realized with horror. It wasn't just Zelna's voice, it was her own ....

"Libby, stop! You've got to do it!" screamed Ginny, and the distraction helped Libby clear her head. She was immediately brought back to the present, and she could have sworn that, for just a split second, when she glanced up at Zelna, it was herself she had seen.

"No!" she shouted, and her hand grasped the handle of her slingshot, pulling it from the pocket of her backpack. Her other hand reached in and grabbed one of the dried berries—there were four left, she could tell—and slipped it into the sling. She was lifting the sling, now aiming it at Zelna's surprised face, but her thoughts became muddled again, and she wondered what she was doing, and why was she pointing that slingshot at herself? No, it was that annoying girl she should be aiming at, the one who had showed up for no explicable reason ... and her thoughts instantly focused, for she knew that the Solstice would magnify her wish.

Her hand turned. She was propped up on the table now, her arm steady and straight and ready to shoot. Ginny's face was white, and it had a terrified look upon it, and she was screaming something back at her, shaking her head wildly as Iorgu held her fast.

"Shoot it," whispered a voice. *"It is an easy kill!"*

"No, Libby, don't!" screamed Ginny, and there were tears streaming down her cheeks.

Freedom from everything. Freedom to know all that she was capable of, to see the world—to *show* the world—with no one standing in the way! She wouldn't be a freak anymore, she would be wonderful!

"Libby, come back!"

The berry zipped across the cavern. A flash of violet light and then, a shriek filled the air. The dry rattle of wings.

Iorgu staggered, but only half in human form. His stunned face morphed even as he fell, and it was just as it had been that day in the castle tower, only backwards: an enormous raven now crouched before them. Zelna cursed and shouted something incomprehensible, but the raven only screeched in response, mad with pain. The wings rustled loudly, a few violent flaps, and with a terrifying cry, the raven darted right into the moonlight, higher and higher through the opening of the cavern until it disappeared into the night far above.

Libby collapsed on the table, exhausted. She could barely move; her arms felt like heavy sand bags. She lay perfectly still, staring up at Zelna, who choked with fury, but to Libby, the room was suddenly calm. It was almost as if she could see her life pass before her, and what she saw was a chance to make it whatever she wanted. She saw Ginny and her parents and Uncle Frank and Buttercup. Her life was far more free than any of those visions of power, she realized; she was free to choose, to be a girl, to grow up to become anything at all. She knew now what it was that she *truly* wanted, and she knew also that her mind was her own, something Zelna could never control, not unless she let her.

"Ginny," she called, but her voice came out in a gasp, wringing the last of her strength from her. "Throw the necklace!"

Ginny blinked back at her, dazed, before her words finally registered, and then everything happened at once. Ginny pulled off the chain from around her neck, slipping the cloth satchel from the stone, and immediately, the moonstone tore from her grasp, shooting across the cavern like a rocket flame—straight at Libby—burning a blue line of light through the air. Libby squeezed her eyes shut, bracing herself.

The explosion was deafening.

Light burst everywhere as the blast threw her from the table. A burning, cold sensation unlike anything Libby had ever felt seared through her. Stone shattering all around, dust filtering with the moonlight, and she gasped for air as a thunderous roar shook the very ground where she lay.

The roar grew louder until it seemed to actually go through her, swirling with the moonlight, howling and pulsing so that Libby heaved on the ground, incapable of controlling the contortions. But it wasn't enough, she knew it; she could still feel the struggle between them. She couldn't breathe, and then she was seeing things, because through the dusty light, she saw the pale form of her mother appear, standing stooped but determined, shouting words Libby had never heard with a fury that sounded as if they were torn from hell itself. More shrieks and smoke mushroomed where the blue light had exploded, and it couldn't be, but her mother fell back, crumpling onto the floor.

Libby rolled on the ground, she could barely see, but through the smoke, the form of Zelna shrieked again, the debris of the shattered stones floating around her in the moonlight, flicking shards of blazing blue, and then the shards sucked in, vibrating with intensity, before they burst out in a violent surge.

Through the roar of this final explosion, a wild howl could be heard, followed by a blinding light, shooting flaming tendrils into the space above so that, from where Libby lay, the entire cavern became a blazing kaleidoscope; fantastic shapes filled her sight, polished shafts twisting and swallowing each other through the roar, and then it swirled and swirled and swirled until it reached the cave's opening far above, sucking the air from everything as it flicked, howling, into the sky.

Libby lay on her back, staring up at the opening. No, that was just a trick of light, she thought, but then there was utter silence, the moonlight dissolved into the night, and far above her, twinkled two of the brightest stars she had ever seen.

She would never forget that stillness, that feeling of profound peace, as if she had been removed from space and time, just floating in the darkness beneath those stars.

It all changed in the next moment, for the cavern suddenly echoed with shouting, and Ginny's voice was joined by others.

"They're gone!" she heard her gasping, "The man and Zelna, they're both gone!"

It was a mass of confusion, but somewhere in the blur, Libby realized that it wasn't just Zelna and Iorgu that were gone. *Everything* was; there was nothing left—not even rubble from the stone table—her slingshot and backpack and everything in it were nowhere to be seen.

She didn't have long to ponder this, however, because she heard Wolfgang's voice barreling off the cavern walls, followed by a determined honk. At the same time, far above her, a flutter of darkness eclipsed the twinkling starlight. She heard Ginny sobbing, but then Wolfgang was saying something to her, and Libby knew everything was going to be alright.

❀

Sunlight beamed through the branches of bare oaks and glowed off the thick, green pines that surrounded the hospital garden. In this manicured clearing, it was hard to believe they were actually smack dab in the center of Hanau. Wolfgang and Ginny had left a few minutes ago to resume their search for Sal, and thanks to the uncommonly warm weather, the nurse had permitted Libby and her parents to stay outdoors a while longer.

Mrs. Frye sat in a wheelchair, wrapped in a thick quilt, complaining about not being allowed to walk on her own yet. And if it were not for the very strange, wide streak of white that ran from the roots of her normally jet-black hair all the way down to the tips, it would have looked as if she'd just awoken from a perfectly normal night of sleep, as healthy and vibrant as ever.

Libby sat across from her, also swaddled in blankets, and her dad sat between them. He was the only one of the three who wasn't an actual patient—a fact that annoyed her mom for some particular reason.

Libby blinked into the sunlight, relieved to be outside. She hated hospitals! She smiled, closing her eyes for a moment, and when she opened them again, she could have sworn that the knotty oak directly in front of her had shifted its branches, so that it looked like it was actually grinning back at her! Libby shook herself.

"Almost forgot! Someone brought this for you," said her dad, fumbling in his pocket. He pulled out a little package and handed it to her. It was wrapped in crumpled tissue paper, tied with a slightly soiled, red ribbon. A note was tucked just underneath.

Libby unfolded it, staring down at the words.

"What's the matter?" he asked.

Libby handed the note to her dad, who read it out loud:

*"Here's to natures that cannot be suppressed,
and to others that need encouraging."*

He handed the note back.

"Sabine?"

"It must be," replied Libby.

"That's what Wolfgang suspected," said her mom. "You should have seen the look on his face when he brought it in from Reception!"

"Ginny told us about the potion while you were sleeping," added her dad, and Libby looked at the note in her hands, feeling rather bewildered by it all. The memory of Sabine was so confusing and far away.

Now that she was back with her parents, it felt too incredible to have really happened to her. But she remembered that dark, frosty morning, just before dawn, when she had stumbled into the cottage at the abbey ruins, terrified and desperate for help. She remembered the exact moment when she first saw Sabine, her horrific face glaring down at her in that fire-lit room and then, in the next moment, everything she knew about life—about herself—had changed. *Everything.* Had it only been a little over a day ago? It should be impossible, so much had happened since. But no, she recalled, thinking it over: They'd been brought in late last night and it was now the afternoon of the next day, so that meant, incredibly, she had first met Sabine less than forty-eight hours before!

"She warned me, though. She said she didn't know if she could trust herself ...."

"Warned you or not, she still risked *your* life, all for the sake of that potion," scowled her mom.

"But she helped us," insisted Libby, feeling defensive for Sabine. "I mean, I couldn't have done it without her. And she saved Buttercup's life."

Her parents didn't appear convinced.

"Well, in any case, you're safe now, and that's what matters," concluded her dad. "We're just relieved to have you. What you did was extraordinary and very brave ... and it terrifies us both!"

"After all you've been through, you must have so many questions," added her mom.

Libby looked from one to the other, unsure of how to respond. It was the first time they had ever talked to her this way! She decided she'd better take advantage while it lasted.

"Well you could tell me how you suddenly appeared in the cave; I've been wondering about that," she suggested to her mom hopefully, but her dad immediately laughed out loud, shaking his head.

"We meant when we got back home! You barely have the strength to walk, and here you are, ready to relive it all again!"

"But it's fair to expect some answers now," said her mom, her brows creasing with concern. "Although *that's* one that requires far more than a fifteen minute hospital break. For now, you should know that it wasn't all me, not entirely."

"But I saw what you did!"

"You saw what I did, true, but not how. It was *you* who enabled the last of it, Libby. You're the one who channeled the Solstice, and much more than that, I suspect."

Libby looked down at her hands, feeling rattled by the memory—of her mom falling to the ground, and then all of that light ..... She shuddered and traced a finger over the tissue paper of her gift. It felt like a small book inside, she guessed, and what was more, she suspected she knew what *kind* of book. She wasn't sure if her parents would approve.

"And the words?" whispered Libby. "Where did you learn that?"

Her mom's brows drew even more tightly together. She shrugged, shaking her head in bemusement. "I've no idea," she admitted. "It was almost like I was reciting something someone else knew."

"Someone like Zelna," considered Libby, recalling what Sabine had explained about the Coven of Hessen, and just the sound of that name made her stomach squeeze. "What do you think happened to her after the explosion?"

The distant expression on her mother's face vanished.

"I've been thinking about that, too – it's impossible to know. Whatever happened in those last few moments, one thing is evident: you were far stronger than she expected, than any of us expected."

Libby cringed at the memory, not feeling strong in the least.

"And Grandmother?" she asked. "What about her?"

Her parents exchanged more glances.

Her dad cleared his throat. "So long as that fortune is no

longer within reach, we don't think she'll be a danger to anyone else. There's not anything else we can do, really."

"But I almost wish she could have had that book," said her mom, and there was a sadness in her eyes that made Libby wish she hadn't brought it up. "If I'd known, I think I would have given it to her gladly, years ago. It must be terrible to live your life for only one thing and never obtain it." She sighed and glanced down at her hands for a moment. When she looked back up at Libby, her expression had changed. She smiled and said, "But that isn't what your dad and I wanted to say to you here. We've got a lot to sort through, the three of us. And the first step is to admit that, in our effort to protect you, we've put you in greater danger and more than that, we've tried to make you believe you were something you're not—that we're all something we're not."

"Although it should be noted that out of the three of us, I'm definitely the most normal," her dad interjected.

"Matter of perspective," sniffed her mom, and then she laughed softly, and it was the warmest, happiest feeling Libby could ever imagine. Her dad chuckled and put his arms out, pulling them both towards him.

"Well, in any case, what we are trying to say, kiddo, is that from now on, we're not going to keep things hidden."

"So does that mean you'll teach me?" asked Libby, and it all came out in a jumble. "I know Mom still, er, … *practices*. I found some of your hidden recipes once in the closet! That's why Uncle Frank always feels so much younger on his birthdays, isn't it? And all those older people you bake for, and the sick ones, too—they always get better. It's your cakes and cookies and stuff, those special herbs!"

For a moment, Gretchen Frye drew back, speechless with surprise. She glanced sheepishly up at Libby's dad, whose arms had just dropped to his sides in genuine astonishment—almost as if he hadn't known about it, either. Libby, on the other hand, could hardly believe her good fortune. All of these questions that had haunted her for so long, and here she was, chatting about them with her parents and actually getting answers! Well, sort of. But her elation faded just as quickly as it came.

"What's the matter?"

Libby frowned, feeling strangely disoriented as she sat back up. She hadn't realized it, but she must have doubled over; her hands were still wrapped around her head.

"What is it, Libby?" pressed her mom. Libby tried to ignore the strange, nauseating throb at her temples, almost like motion-sickness, and she didn't understand it, but it felt as if her eyes were actually swelling, so that she had to squeeze them shut. At least she knew it would go away in a moment; it had already happened once before, a few hours after arriving at the hospital.

"It's more like remembering," she struggled to explain, but it was hard to find the right words. "When the blue light surrounds Zelna, and it feels like something is being … well, I'm not sure, but it feels like something's being *pulled* from me."

"Like what?" whispered her mother.

"It's like a vacuum," she answered slowly, keeping her eyes closed to see the picture in her mind. "It fills the entire space around the crushed table, and I'm lying in the middle of it all—it's that last bit I remember the most clearly. I remember runes on the ground, strange shapes and symbols I didn't notice before, and when it comes back to me, I get this disorienting feeling, like I'm going to throw up, but it's coming from my *eyes* for some weird reason—or from behind them, maybe. It's happening slower each time, and it's like a new detail is seen, like I'm inside that vacuum of light, seeing it all sucked up, slower and slower, and I'm not able to follow it—I'm just laying there and I keep wondering why. Why did it take away everything but leave us? And why do I keep *seeing* it?"

Just as their eyes met, her mother turned away, taking a sudden interest in the quilt patches of her blanket. Libby turned to her dad, who quickly glanced from her to her mom, and she could see by the look on his face that there was something they weren't telling her. He reached over and took her hand instead.

"Like your mom said, we've got a lot to discuss, the three of us. Let's just get home safely first, shall we? We'll have all our lives to sort out the rest."

And they couldn't have timed it better, because before Libby could protest, the nurse marched up the narrow path toward them, tapping her watch in disapproval.

21

AN UNEXPECTED REUNION

I t felt like an eternity, but it was only a week before they were finally on their way back home. How Wolfgang managed to explain Ginny's situation to the German authorities, Libby never could fully account for, but he had and that was all that mattered. Even Buttercup was permitted a compartment on the plane!

But the most wonderful part of all was seeing Uncle Frank's face when their rickety station wagon pulled up to his house.

His mobile unit could not move fast enough. It didn't help that, in his excitement, he kept switching gears between hover-mode and wheels, which only confused matters and made Esmerelda laugh hysterically—a very annoying thing to hear.

Even so, he still met them at the driveway before they'd had a chance to open the doors. And then they were all hugging and laughing and crying at the same time—even Uncle Frank.

Ginny told most of the story, and Libby thought that a few details might have been slightly embellished. Still, she had to admit it made things far more interesting, although she couldn't recall half of the events and she was certain she had never *levitated* in the air right before she raised her slingshot—she would have remembered that! But that was how Ginny told it, her eyes wide with wonder.

"In the light, it was all so confusing," she continued, looking at them all as if she could see it happening as she spoke. "But Libby was definitely floating up from the table, towards that woman Zelna. And just when I thought it couldn't get any stranger, they started …." She stopped, fixating on the ground.

"What? They started what?" prompted Uncle Frank.

Ginny squirmed, glancing nervously at Libby.

"It's okay Ginny, tell us what you saw," said Libby, trying to smile encouragingly, but that same, sickening feeling suddenly came back, and she had to turn away for a moment.

"Well, I don't know how else to say it, but they were *blending*," blurted Ginny, and then everything tumbled out of her mouth at once. "Libby and Zelna were somehow combining together! That's when I realized what Zelna had meant when she said that her price was Libby—she meant it literally! It looked like she was … *dissolving* into Libby, I guess—and in the next second, all I could see of her was a line of light, like she had absorbed into her somehow, and when Libby turned and pointed that slingshot right at me, I could see it in her face," Ginny's eyes grew even wider and her voice fell to nearly a whisper. "It was the scariest thing I've ever seen! It was so *cold*, and I knew that it wasn't my friend anymore who was looking at me!"

Libby shuddered. For just an instant, the thrill of that moment came over her again, and she remembered the power of it, so terrifying and tempting ....

Ginny was now looking at everyone, her face growing more and more animated. "I was screaming and then Libby was fighting it, and you could see her coming back outside that light, and in the next instant, Zelna was alone again! It all happened so quickly, but I could see their faces, just before Libby turned to that man who was holding me and shot him!"

Another shudder went down Libby's spine, and that nauseating throb nearly blinded her, and for a brief moment, she wondered what would have happened if she'd given in; she had been so close. But no, she shook herself, she knew the answer already, she could feel it, like a borrowed memory, something foreign but belonging, like recalling a dream....

"That was all thanks to you, Ginny," she grappled, trying to concentrate on the present. "You're the one who reminded me about the slingshot."

"But that only got rid of the man," said Ginny, clearly relieved to finally be talking about it. "If Libby hadn't thought of the necklace, there's no way we would've gotten out of there alive! As soon as I let it go, there was this terrible flash of light—you couldn't see anything—until suddenly, Mrs. Frye was there, just appearing out of nowhere!"

"Which is the most excitement I wish to have in a very, very long time," interrupted Gretchen Frye, watching Libby with a rather worried expression. "But enough of this talk. We need to celebrate being back together as a family!"

"Including one Ginevieve Rae Gonzalez," added Libby, and Ginny beamed, forgetting all about her story.

"I can hardly believe it myself!" she giggled. "I bet Mr. Snookles had to take an extra shot of whisky when he heard the news!"

Uncle Frank threw a confused look his nephew's way.

"We're petitioning for custody," grinned Libby's dad.

"Why, Ginny, that's wonderful!" cried Uncle Frank, and Esmerelda nodded enthusiastically in agreement. Libby tried to match the celebratory mood, but her thoughts were drifting back through those events in the cave again, and the harder she tried *not* to dwell on it, the more she did....

"What's the matter, Sassafras?"

"Oh, nothing," she fibbed, trying to look cheerful.

"Well, I for one could not be happier!" exclaimed Uncle Frank, but then his attention turned to something else altogether. Libby looked in the direction of his gaze and saw a figure emerging from the trees, now stalking up the driveway towards them.

"Holy Macaroni," gasped Ginny.

The figure halted a few feet away, hands on hips. He was dressed in overalls and tall, white rubber boots. A few dried shrimp tails clung to his clothes while a swarm of flies buzzed around his head. He swatted at one irritably.

"Sal!" cried Ginny, recovering from her shock, and then she was lunging toward him and hugging him around the middle. "Oh, gross, you really stink!"

"What'd you expect!"

"Where ... where's your plane?" blurted Uncle Frank.

"I just crossed hell's half acre to get here, and *that's* the first thing you've got to say to me? You've got no inkling what I've gone through!" Sal glared, and then he grew distracted by the beautiful woman with the strange, white stripe of hair staring back at him.

"But how did you get here?" gasped Ginny. "We looked for you all over Hanau—we thought ...."

"Thought ole Sal had bit the dust, did you? Well, you're not far off the mark, kid, because after I dropped you off, I was chased out of the darn county!"

"Those jets!" exclaimed Ginny. "They didn't catch you, did they?"

Sal glanced from Ginny to the pretty lady who was still staring at him, and he straightened his stance, puffing out his chest a little. "Catch Sal McCool? Course not! When it comes to flying, I can out-loop, out-smart and out-think any son-of-a-gun, German or no! Pardon my French, ma'am."

"But—"

"Like I was saying, I was flying like heck over the Atlantic with blood pressure up to here," he paused to make the appropriate gesture, "leaving those jets in a tizzy, I was, and what happens? I get caught in a storm where I can hardly see a thing! Feared for my life, and that's saying something. And as I was piloting that jalopy through the stormy skies, *of all things*, I get attacked by a *giant bird*. Must have been as big as me! With the weather and all, I thought at first it was another plane; I swerved to miss it and wouldn't you know it, lost control." Sal glared testily at Uncle Frank. "Down I went, into the stormy sea. Thought that was all she wrote and if it makes you feel special, I cursed you, Frank Frye, the whole way down."

Uncle Frank managed to swallow.

"But no," continued Sal, now waggling a finger. "I was too angry to even die! As fate would have it, I got picked up by an Irish fisherman an hour later who brought me to shore and hooked me up with a friend of his brother-in-law who has a cousin who just happened to be leaving that week for New Orleans. Cargo pilot." Sal spat a stream of tobacco juice on the ground. "Beautiful country there, by the way. Ireland, that is."

"Isn't-it-though," said Esmerelda agreeably. "I-have-seen-pictures."

"What the—" Sal paused and scratched his head, opening and closing his mouth as he stared at the shiny robot. And then, a look of determination came over him, and it was clear that he wasn't even going to let a beautiful woman with two-toned hair and a chatty robot distract him. "So anyway, I finally landed in New Orleans and I hitched a ride on a shrimp boat headed for Biloxi." Sal paused to swat at the fly swarming about his nose. "Don't know what everyone else's problem was. As soon as I got off that boat, I was avoided like the plague! Only rides I could get were trucks hauling livestock up Highway 49, but it got me here, by golly, and seeing as I've lost my plane and have nowhere to go, I think you'll be gracious enough to spare me a room for a while!"

Uncle Frank blinked again.

Sal shifted his weight. "Well?"

"A *bird?*" said Uncle Frank.

Sal glared off into the distance, the cloud of flies buzzing contentedly about his sunburned head.

"Yeah," he grumbled. "White one. But the strangest thing—after I crashed and found myself floating in the middle of the ocean, that *same* bird came swooping down at me, as if just to spite me. He sat there in the water, honking away. Honked for so loud and so long, I think it's what attracted the fisherman who picked me up. Diabolical fowl, I swear. I mean, what kind of self-respecting goose wears a string of purple beads around its neck? Gave me the willies, it did. I—"

"Buttercup!" exclaimed Uncle Frank.

Sal staggered backwards.

"Who do you think you're talking to? *I* just want a *room!*"

"No, stupid: Buttercup," glared Uncle Frank, pointing at the porch. "A bird as big as you, huh?"

Sal followed Uncle Frank's gesture, and for the first time, noticed Buttercup, who had paused in his march across the mended floorboards and was now honking in friendly acknowledgment. Sal's eyes narrowed, and then he picked a shrimp tail off his sleeve and flicked it away.

"Well, wouldn't you know," he growled, turning to Uncle Frank with a nasty expression. "Only *you* would be capable of setting such a chain of events into motion!"

And with that, Sal stomped past them, marched up the stairs and escorted himself into Uncle Frank's house without another word. It was quiet for a few seconds, and then Ginny began to giggle. Soon everyone but Uncle Frank was laughing.

"Looks like you've got company," snickered Libby's dad.

"Company? More like an invasion!"

"Hey, at least it'll give the girls an extra victim," teased her mom, but Uncle Frank only grunted, still staring despairingly at the front door. "You've been selected as the guinea pig," she continued cheerily. "Wolfgang's going to give baking classes through video chat, so they're counting on you for an unbiased opinion."

Uncle Frank stopped glaring after Sal and glanced between Libby's parents. "Video chat, eh?" he repeated, raising his wiry eyebrows in surprise. "So you two are finally giving Libby access to the world outside?"

"Within reason," chuckled her dad. "I don't think we could have kept it up anyway; she was wearing us out!"

"But now, we're finally free," beamed her mom, wrapping her arms around Libby's shoulders. "We don't have to hide anymore."

And the sound of those words chased away Libby's uneasy feeling. They wouldn't have to hide anymore. No more secrets! For the first time since that day with the yellow envelope, she felt at peace.

Libby looked up at her mom, then at everyone around her, and she knew she had everything that really mattered. She didn't care anymore if she didn't fit in at school or if Julie Lambert and her gang of friends made fun of her. In fact, being different was going to be nothing short of … well, magical.

Her mom immediately stopped smiling.

"I know that expression—what are you thinking?"

"Oh, just that I've got some catching up to do," replied Libby, which was true, of course.

But she wasn't just thinking about going back to school or finally getting answers to all of those questions she still had about her family, or even about mastering the art of Wolfgang's cream cheese danishes. For starters, there was that tin of strange recipes she'd discovered all those months ago, not to mention the little book Sabine had sent to her at the hospital.

Libby grinned up at her mom—and she tried to look as innocent as possible at the notion—because, after all, she had a whole lot of interesting spells to learn ….

ABOUT THE AUTHOR

J. L. McCreedy spent over a year living in Rodenbach, Germany, in the State of Hessen, while preparing the original draft of *Liberty Frye and the Witches of Hessen*.

She first learned a love of writing (and developed an incurable condition of wanderlust) while growing up in Southeast Asia as the child of missionaries. She holds a B.A. in English and a law degree, freelances as a writer and consultant for charitable organizations, and whenever possible, drags her splendid husband on ill-planned adventures. She currently lives in the White Mountains of New Hampshire.

Made in the USA
Columbia, SC
06 November 2018